RASPBERRY TRUFFLE MURDER

A MAPLE HILLS COZY MYSTERY #1

WENDY MEADOWS

MAJESTIC OWL PUBLISHING LLC

1

Dipping her right index finger down into a glass bowl, Nikki Bates swooped up a small amount of freshly stirred dark chocolate mix and nervously sampled the taste. "Relax, Mom," Seth Bates told his mother, setting his backpack down at his feet. Leaning against the kitchen counter lined with bowls of different chocolate mixes, he shook his head. "Here I am off to college, and here you are making delicious chocolate. Now tell me again why I'm about to waste my youth slaving over books when I could help you run your store?"

Allowing the taste of the chocolate to settle in her mouth like a child deciding if she liked the taste of a new candy or not, Nikki studied her son's young and innocent face. Seth came later in life than she'd expected. Here she was, a forty-two-year-old woman, divorced after twenty years of marriage, starting her life fresh and new in a small town in Vermont. And there stood her son, a skinny, nervous and shy young man who was terrified at the idea of leaving home and venturing off into the powerful tides of college. Wiping her black bangs off her forehead, she sighed. Glancing down at the plain, light blue dress, she felt depressed and bland. Although she had once won the beauty pageant in her hometown in Georgia when she was twenty-one, those years now seemed far away, replaced by crow's feet and sadness. "Seth, you have a wonderful scholarship. It's not every day a young man gets a scholarship to one of the most prestigious colleges in the country."

Watching his mother examine her outward appearance like a tired bird wondering which feather to pluck next, Seth lowered his eyes. He didn't like to see his mother so sad, but what could he do? His dad had deserted them for a new life in Los Angeles. Looking down at the jeans he was wearing, he felt helpless. "Will you be okay, Mom? I mean...being alone?"

"Oh, sure," Nikki promised, putting on a brave voice. "Tomorrow is the grand opening of my store, just in time for tourist season. I'm scared, but excited. It's good for me to be here, Seth. I needed away from Georgia...from the memories."

Raising his head, Seth swung his eyes around the kitchen. The kitchen was small but nice, all hardwood. A wooden island with a stove stood in the middle of the kitchen like a welcoming beacon shining from a tall lighthouse. At the end of the kitchen, an oval window hung over the kitchen sink, offering a view to a broad backyard with a wide duck pond. The cabin his mother had purchased, Seth thought, was actually kinda cool. He especially liked the stone fireplace in the living room and the smell of pine emanating from the wood. Maybe his mother would be all right? Maybe college wouldn't be all that bad? Maybe life would go on after all. "Well, my bus leaves in an hour. I guess you better drive me into town, huh?"

"I'm so very proud of you," Nikki told her son. Walking to him, she embraced him. "Someday you're going to become a fine doctor, you just wait and see."

"I might become a dentist instead. With all of this chocolate around, this town might need one," Seth joked.

"Maybe," Nikki joked back, feeling her spirits lift. "Okay, come on, Mr. College-Man, let's get you into town. Today begins the first step of the rest of your life."

After dropping off her son in town, Nikki drove back to her cabin, bawling her eyes out. She had been able to withhold her tears in front of Seth, but as soon as his bus pulled away, the floodgates opened. Her baby boy was grown up. Memories of feedings and diaper changes, smiles that were actually gas, first words, first tooth, whispered in Nikki's mind. She knew from what other mothers told her that the day she sent her son off to college she would cry an ocean of tears. Now that day had come, and here she was, driving down a beautiful country road, crying her ocean of tears. Nikki knew, though, that she was crying over other things. Her divorce had been messy and cruel. Leaving Georgia to begin a new life in Vermont had been extremely difficult.

She felt lost and somehow trapped in a strange new world that she had been thrust into unwillingly. Watching rain begin to tap at the windshield of her white SUV, she clicked on the windshield wipers. "I'll go home and read a book. That's what I'll do," she promised herself. "I'll make myself some hot chocolate and read a good mystery. Tomorrow will be a better day. Life will get back to normal...it has to."

Overhead, dark gray storm clouds settled in over Nikki's cabin and remained until morning.

2

Amazed at how many tourists were in her store, Nikki quickly wiped her hands on a pink apron wrapped around the bright yellow dress she was wearing. Expecting opening day to be a flop, she couldn't believe how busy she had become as soon as she advertised her store was open for business. "My, it's so busy," she told Lidia Green.

"Tourist season," Lidia smiled, watching Nikki quickly tie her long black hair into a ponytail. "Honey, you better pace yourself, or you'll wear yourself down to a nub."

Standing behind chest-high glass counters displaying every kind of chocolate imaginable, Nikki drew in a deep breath. Her store was small and a little cramped, but also warm and safe, filled with the scents of delicious chocolate and freshly brewed coffee. The floors, like those in her cabin, were hardwood, and the walls were decorated with signs and posters advertising chocolates from around the world and from different times. "I guess I'd better," Nikki agreed. She liked Lidia Green from the first moment they had met. Unsure of how to hire people, Nikki had met Lidia while holding job interviews at her store. Lidia had won her heart over like the way vanilla ice cream melts over warm, freshly baked apple pie.

Lidia watched an older couple stop and study a tray of chocolate. At the age of sixty-one, she felt happy and content with her life. She and her husband, Herbert, liked living in Vermont. After pitching their RV at Maple Hills RV Park seven years ago, they had settled in and become part of the local population. At first, her West Virginia ways didn't click too well, but after a while, the townspeople became used to her. Lidia knew that after a while, Nikki, too, would settle in and become just one of the town's people. "I better go check on Tori," she winked at Nikki. "That young girl can get lost in her own car."

Nikki smiled gratefully. She watched Lidia walk away toward the back storeroom wearing a plain white dress that somehow brought out every feature of her aging beauty. Sure, Lidia appeared to be plain-looking with short gray hair, but when Nikki looked deeply into the woman's face, she saw a beautiful angel. "Can I help you?" Nikki asked, turning her attention to the older couple studying the tray of dark German chocolate.

"Yes, can we sample this chocolate?" a woman wearing a dark green shirt over a black dress asked in a German accent, that to Nikki, seemed mingled with a hint of an Austrian accent.

"You sure can." Nikki smiled happily. Her business was

going to be a success. She was going to be okay. Everything was going to work out. The gray cloud hanging over her sad heart would not remain forever.

Hearing the bell hanging over the front door clatter, Nikki looked up from her work and saw a tall, handsome man with dark red hair enter her store. The man, she quickly noticed, was wearing a gray suit and had the appearance of a government agent. He was alone. His face was hard and stone-like. Nikki watched him examine her store, focus his attention on her customers, and then turn and leave. "How strange," she whispered, feeling her chest tighten.

"What's strange?" Tori Russ asked.

"Oh," Nikki said, startled, "I was just..." Unsure of how to proceed, Nikki placed two small pieces of the dark German chocolate onto a paper plate with a floral design. Handing the plate to the German woman, she smiled. "Please, enjoy."

"Thank you," the German woman smiled back.

Turning her attention to Tori, Nikki sighed. There, standing next to her was a delicate and beautiful twenty-year-old woman who had the prettiest blond hair and blue eyes she had ever seen. Tori reminded Nikki of a young Lana Turner. The only problem was that Tori wasn't confident in her beauty or herself. The young woman was always holding her head down, barely wanting to interact with customers, always finding some chore to do first. Instead of wearing a pretty dress, she wore a long white t-shirt over a pair of baggy jeans. Tori broke Nikki's heart. "Dear, can you please help these nice people?" she asked, hoping Tori would accept her suggestion.

Tori nervously eyed the old couple and reluctantly nodded her head. She needed the job and was grateful that Nikki had hired her. Living with her Aunt wasn't the greatest, but a home was a home, and she needed money. "I guess...yes, ma'am."

Hearing the bells hanging over the front door clang and clatter again, Nikki saw Lidia's husband, Herbert, quickly enter the store, wiping sweat from his face. Herbert hurried to the front counter, braking hard. With shaky hands, he fiddled with the brown toupee on his bald head and then looked around for his wife. "Where's Lidia?"

"Is something the matter?" Nikki asked, reading the tension and worry in Herbert's face. She knew Herbert was a retired car salesman. The man, she learned, could sell dirt to a worm; his appearance was natural and calm, intelligent and focused. Now, though, he seemed in an outright state of panic.

Glancing over his shoulder toward the front door, Herbert wiped his sweaty hands on the brown t-shirt he was wearing. "I was walking to your store to see Lidia when I saw a man crossing Cloud Street. And out of nowhere, a black SUV came plowing down the street and ran him down."

"Oh dear!" Nikki gasped, placing her hands to her mouth. Hearing the bells on the front door jingling again, she looked at the door just in time to see the old German couple leave.

"Herbert," Lidia said, walking up behind Nikki, "it's not lunch time yet."

"No time for lunch," Herbert told his wife and explained to her what he had told Nikki. "Just like that, hit and run..."

"Did you see the driver?" Nikki ventured to ask. Feeling her inner detective waking up, she allowed her eyes to wander to the spot in the store where the old German couple had been standing. The sounds of distant sirens approaching filled the empty space, which caused the remaining customers in the store to hurry outside.

"That will be Chief Daily," Herbert rolled his eyes. "The man couldn't figure out which end of a ruler to use," he complained.

"What's happening?" Tori asked, walking up to Lidia.

"A hit-and-run, it seems," Lidia explained. "Herbert, you saw the SUV, so you better go talk to Chief Daily."

"Why? All I saw was a black SUV. I'm sure other people saw it. There wasn't a tag. That was the first thing I looked for. The windows were tinted too dark to see the driver," Herbert fussed. "I'm not going to waste my time talking to that old grouch and have him drill me. Oh, he would just love that. No way, no ma'am."

"No tag—are you sure?" Nikki asked Herbert. Suddenly the smell of chocolate in her store that had once been warm and inviting had become tainted by murder.

"I'm sure," Herbert said, trying to regain his natural composure, but Nikki noticed the poor man was deeply shaken.

In Nikki's mind, she saw the tall, handsome man wearing the gray suit enter her store, study her customers, and then leave. "The man who was run down, Herbert...what was he wearing?"

"Why, a gray suit. Why?" Herbert asked.

Nikki didn't answer. Instead, she focused her attention on the front door of her store.

3

Sitting in the back office, Nikki shuffled through a stack of vendor orders, trying to focus. The hit-and-run in town was distracting her. It all seemed so strange. The killing, obviously intentional, didn't sit well against the backdrop of a small and cozy Vermont town. *No,* Nikki thought as she tossed the vendor orders down onto an antique wooden desk she had picked up in Northern New York at an antique shop. The killing had nothing to do with her new town or its people...or so it seemed at that moment. The killing, Nikki continued thinking, standing up from a white and pink wooden chair, must have been carried out by an outsider. The victim just happened to be in her new hometown, that's all.

Pacing around the small, cramped office, Nikki walked to a wooden filing cabinet, studied a blue basket holding cinnamon-scented potpourri, and then focused her attention on the burgundy walls. "The man looked straight at the old German couple," she said aloud, forcing her mind to walk down paths of logical reasoning. "He looked straight at them and then walked out of the store. Then when Herbert announced the hit-and-run, the couple left. Is there a possible connection?"

Hearing the white door to the office open, Nikki watched Lidia walk in. "Well, life in this small town just got a bit more interesting."

"What do you mean?" Nikki asked.

Easing the office door shut, Lidia motioned Nikki over to her. "Honey, the man who was killed was Steven Denforth."

Nikki shook her head, confused. "Lidia, I'm new in town, remember?"

"Oh, yes, that's right," Lidia quickly apologized. Pulling Nikki over to the desk, she asked her to sit down. "I'll explain."

"Please do," Nikki pressed.

"One year ago, a man from Manhattan bought the local paper here. No one has ever seen him. I didn't even know the paper had changed hands until Tori told me, and she found out from her aunt. Anyway, all of a sudden, the paper begins printing these poisonous stories about local people...horrible stuff, but all protected under our First Amendment rights. So what can people do? The stories continue, tempers flare, calls to shut down the paper are made to the Mayor. But nothing is done."

"Why didn't people stop buying the newspaper?" Nikki inquired.

"That would have been the smart path to take," Lidia told Nikki, nodding her head vigorously, "but in defense of the town, no one knew who was going to be Denforth's next target. Now here is where we begin walking in real dirty water."

Nikki slowly folded her arms. She felt a sudden craving for a cup of coffee and a square of fudge, but she waited for Lidia to continue. "I'm ready."

"Well," Lidia said, glancing at the office door, suddenly nervous, "finally a meeting was arranged at the town hall after someone made threats to run the mayor out of town... Who, I really don't know. All I know is our money-hungry mayor realized that votes count, and he had better make an appearance and listen to the concerned voices of those who voted for him. So the meeting took place, and it wasn't long before tempers erupted, and the air became very heated. People were demanding that the mayor give them answers. How was the paper getting personal information on them? Who was Steven Denforth? Oh, yelling matches like you've never seen hit the floor running. And then, out of nowhere, the mayor shouts, 'Maybe it's one of the citizens in town giving the paper information?'"

"Ah," Nikki said, nodding, "he was in the hot seat, so he conveniently turned the tables. But it also seems like the mayor was protecting Steven Denforth."

Lidia opened the office door, peeped out into an empty store, and closed the door. "It did seem like the mayor was standing as a wall between Steven Denforth and the people of our fair town. But," Lidia sighed, "that fact was quickly swept under the carpet. When the mayor screamed that it could be one of our own feeding information to an outsider, well...let's just say that the shouting stopped and the sounds of crickets began. People began looking at each other; suddenly everyone became a suspect."

"Divide and conquer?" Nikki asked.

"Maybe," Lidia explained. "After the meeting, the unity holding the people of this town together for a single cause went down the drain. As I said, everyone became a suspect. People stopped trusting each other."

"But the stories continued," Nikki said.

"For a while," Lidia nodded, "maybe a month more, but then, someone set the building the paper was housed in on fire. All in all, the whole incident lasted for about six months."

"Oh," Nikki sat up in her chair, her excitement running a race with her curiosity, "Any arrests?"

"Not a one," Lidia said, lowering her voice down to a barely audible whisper, "but word got around that whoever torched the paper was a professional. The fire didn't spread, and let me tell you, that building is squeezed between two other buildings, so the fire should have spread like a virus."

"I see," Nikki said, evaluating every word Lidia had revealed to her, "but I still get the local paper at home."

"I guess whoever burned Steven Denforth out got his message across, because Denforth sold out to Benjamin Westmore and, well, that was the last of it...until today," Lidia said, scratching the back of her head. "Town hasn't really ever been the same since. Oh, people aren't at each other's throats like they used to be, but when the trust shared by a small town is broken..."

"I understand," Nikki assured Lidia, thinking back on her divorce. "Well," she said, standing up and taking a deep breath, "it looks like I need to make a trip to the library. And I need your assistance."

"What for?"

"I need to go to the archives. I need a beginning date, when the first story began, and when the last story was printed. I also need the names of everyone Denforth trashed in his paper," Nikki explained.

"Oh, dear," Lidia said nervously, "I don't know. You might stir up a sleeping hornets' nest. Please understand, if you're going to make it in this town, you need the support of the locals. Herbert and I live out at the campground, but we understand that our welcome mat, even at the campground, can be yanked out from under us in a hurry. You're new here...I don't think it's wise to shake the nest of the elders, so to speak."

"Lidia," Nikki said, holding her ground, "a man has been murdered. I will conduct my own private investigation, very quietly. Back home, on certain cases, Detective Dalton used to request my help. You see," Nikki hesitantly confessed, "my father was an FBI agent. Oh, he was the best. He taught me practically everything I know about solving crimes."

"You were a cop?" Lidia asked, examining Nikki's beautiful and soft features.

"Well, no," Nikki smiled bashfully. "I met my ex-husband when I was twenty-two. I was preparing to go to the academy to become an FBI agent, but Andrew—my ex-husband—changed the course of my life. About...oh, two or three months before I was due to leave for the academy, I was out jogging through the historic downtown district. I always enjoyed jogging in the early morning hours. So peaceful. Birds singing, fresh, cool, morning air, flowers waking up."

"Sounds very nice," Lidia agreed, listening to Nikki with care. "But..."

"But," Nikki sighed, "I came to the end of the street and decided to cross over to the other side and jog back home. So, I began to cross over, and the next thing I know I'm lying in the street holding my ankle in pain."

"You tripped?"

"I can't rightly say," Nikki confessed. "A man named Mr. Green was nearby. He was opening his restaurant—you know, the kind that serves breakfast and lunch only." Lidia nodded, motioning to Nikki that she knew that type of restaurant. "He was an old man, but he sure made it over to me in record time. After examining my ankle, he insisted on taking me to the emergency room. I have to say, as much pain as I was in, I didn't put up much of a fuss."

"Did you break your ankle?"

"Oh no," Nikki explained, "a severe sprain was the diagnosis. Which leads me to my ex-husband. He was the attending ER doctor at the hospital that morning. Oh, I believed it was love at first sight. And maybe, for a few years, it was."

Hearing pain and grief strike Nikki's voice, Lidia hurried over to her. Putting warm, loving hands around her shoulders, she squeezed Nikki. "A broken heart takes time, dear. Now, let's forget this whole business of going to the library and—"

"No," Nikki politely interrupted, "even though I never

attended the Academy, I did get my degree in journalism. My husband ended up moving to Atlanta, and I landed a job on the paper. That's where I met Detective Dalton. I sure was a thorn in his side at first, but after he found out I was the daughter of Famed FBI Agent Henry Bates, he softened up on me some...or maybe my father gave him a call?"

Lidia smiled. "Fathers do make calls."

Nikki thought of her ex-husband. "My ex-husband was spending many hours at the hospital. I was spending many hours at the paper. We became strangers passing in the night. Our son became our anchor. But I knew we were falling out of love; I simply refused to believe it. And when Detective Dalton started asking me to help him on certain cases, oh, I became consumed. I guess it was as much my fault as it was my ex-husband's. We both stopped putting effort into being married, and we focused on our son."

"But it still hurts," Lidia told Nikki.

"Yes, because I did truly love my ex-husband at one time in my life. We shared so many special memories together...memories lost," Nikki sighed painfully.

"I'm sorry, dear. But I still don't see why you're insisting on stirring the hornets' nest here?"

"I regret to admit this, but after what you have told me, I believe the murder involves this town and everyone in it, including me. I'm new here, remember? When people learn about my past, that I worked for a newspaper in Atlanta, all eyes might be on me. At this point, once again, everyone is a suspect. It's obvious that Steven Denforth didn't leave our quaint little town, and someone knew it," Nikki explained. "That someone might end up being made out to be...well, yours truly. I have to investigate this murder to protect myself."

"Oh dear," Lidia said uneasily. Staring at the office door, she considered Nikki's suggestion. "Okay, I'll go to the library with you. I don't know how much help I can be, but I'll try."

Grabbing her purse off the desk, Nikki looked straight at Lidia with determination. "This Steven Denforth walked into the store, looked around at the customers, focused on an old German couple, and then walked out. Afterward, he was run down and killed. Any help you can give me will be greatly appreciated."

4

Opening her purse, Nikki took out a pair of stylish reading glasses. Sitting in a cushioned chair in a small but convenient reading room, she put on the glasses and focused on the newspapers sitting on the table before her. "A total of five stories," she told Lidia.

Sitting across from Nikki, Lidia eased her eyes around the room nervously. "Just pretend you're reading the papers. If anyone gets wise to us, we're sure to be tarred and feathered."

"The door is shut," Nikki said, glancing at the door separating the reading room from the library. "Mrs. Slokam was nice enough. She didn't seem the least bit suspicious."

Watching Nikki pick up a newspaper and examine the front page with intelligent and curious eyes, Lidia tried to relax. It was one thing to have a murder in town; it was a completely different side of the coin to be sitting in a reading room investigating the murder. *Oh pooh*, Lidia fussed at herself, she wasn't investigating any murder. She was simply assisting a friend with research...at least that was the story she was going to stick to if questioned. "Is there anything I can do to help?"

"The people written about, do they still reside here?" Nikki asked, opening the newspaper.

"As far as I know," Lidia answered, "I'm not aware of anyone leaving, but I live out at the campground and don't keep track of everybody's coming and going."

"Fair enough," Nikki told Lidia, focusing on the 'Around Town' section. "This is the section each story was printed in. The first person is...Dr. Ronald Mayton."

Lidia felt her stomach tighten. She was certain the door leading into the reading room was going to burst open at any minute, and a flood of people was going to run into the room screaming at her with furious faces. "Ronald Mayton is Mr. Boss over at the hospital. He's a lousy doctor who can't even stitch up a cut finger properly," she explained, staring at the door.

"The article reads: 'The heartbeat of a small town cannot properly function without a strong medical facility staffed with confident, skilled, educated personnel obedient to the life-saving task of providing quality medical care. Yes, a medical facility skilled at patient care is the heart that pumps blood into a small town. So what does Maple Hills have? Oh my, the mere thought of confessing the messy and ugly truth about our little hospital makes me wish I could infect myself with an infectious disease and run to rabid dogs for treatment instead of our esteemed Doctor Ronald Mayton. Our little hospital is an open morgue in itself, but do we really have to add to the horror by adding an incompetent imbecile to the list of uneducated staff members who have difficulty understanding how to read your blood pressure?

'Oh yes, I am talking about you, Dr. Mayton. In the town of Maple Hills, you stroll around, esteemed and honored, your head arrogantly in the air, waving, smiling, pretending to be someone you're not. You self-righteous little man, filled with dark lies. How is it, Dr. Mayton, that you, a man who beats his wife and smokes illegal drugs, hold a position as a physician? I suppose you have learned a trick or two over the years, though, right? Sure you have. You know how to make sure the bruises you inflict on your wife appear only under her clothes and that the drug tests you take somehow—very tidily by the way—come back very clean, even though you have a basement full of drugs...'"

Lidia looked at Nikki. "Why did you stop reading?"

"Talk about vicious," Nikki whispered. "This article is libelous. Dr. Mayton would have every right to sue."

"Keep reading," Lidia sighed.

Nikki finished the article. At the bottom was a list of sources to support each harsh claim against Ronald Mayton. "Arrest records, court records, dates, names of judges..."

"Ronald Mayton has lived very quietly in our little town for ten years. He moved here from Boston," Lidia explained. "I'm surprised he's still employed at the hospital."

"I wonder if all the charges against him were dropped?" Nikki asked. Pulling out a pen and notepad from her purse, she scribbled down a few notes and then moved on to the next paper. However, before she could throw her eyes onto the article, someone knocked at the reading room door.

Nervously, Lidia stood up, walked to the door, and slowly opened it. "I'm sorry," a tall, thin lady with squiggly gray hair told Lidia, "but I'm afraid I must ask for the newspapers back."

"Why?" Lidia asked Mrs. Slokam, examining the woman's face as quickly as she could. Mrs. Slokam was a pleasant woman. Always wearing brightly colored dresses and happy smiles, she never had a cruel or unfair word to say about anyone. She and her husband attended the local church and participated in food drives and every charity event imaginable. An outstanding member of the community, or so it seemed. Now the woman stood facing her with a determined face. "Lidia, I'm not a foolish woman. I can't deny anyone access to the newspapers in this library. But I know what editions your friend asked for. I called Chief Daily. He instructed me to lock up the editions in question."

Lidia bit down on her lower lip. Glancing over her shoulder, she saw Nikki stand up. Very calmly Nikki walked to the door. "Ma'am, if you try to take these newspapers away from me, I will be forced to contact my attorney. At this point, all I have is your word that you contacted a law enforcement official who instructed you to remove the newspapers from my possession. However, you do not have any proof. Now, I'm sure you're a wonderful woman, and that you are telling the truth, but I must ask for proof that Chief Daily has instructed you to remove these newspapers. Please, go get the proof and I will remain here. The newspapers will not leave this room."

Mrs. Slokam eyed Nikki carefully. "You are forcing me to ask Chief Daily to come here in person," she warned Nikki. "Please, let's resolve this situation without it becoming more than it needs to be."

"I'm sorry," Nikki said, pulling Lidia away from the door, "I must insist that you present me with evidence. I'll be waiting." Nikki closed the door to the reading room and rushed to her purse. Pulling out her cell phone, she asked for Lidia's help. "Start opening the papers to the stories. I need photos."

"Oh my," Lidia said with shaky hands, "you are getting me into trouble."

"I have a plan. Please, just help me," Nikki begged.

"Okay," Lidia caved in. For several minutes she opened each paper, allowing Nikki to take a single photo of each story. When the last photo was taken, Nikki grabbed Lidia's hand and rushed her out into the library. Walking over the pale green carpet, she approached the check-out desk. "Mrs. Slokam, my friend here has convinced me that I was in the wrong. She has told me so many wonderful things about you. Please forgive me for being so stubborn. The papers are in the reading room, neatly folded on the table."

A gentle smile of relief washed over Mrs. Slokam's face. She told Nikki to forget their little disagreement and that she would call Chief Daily and have him cancel his trip to the library. "You seem like a very pleasant person," she said to Nikki. "Perhaps the next time you pay our library a visit we can talk and become more acquainted."

"Without newspapers," Nikki joked.

"Of course," Mrs. Slokam agreed without even wondering what Nikki wanted with the papers, and even how she knew about the papers to begin with, for that matter. After all, Nikki was still a stranger in town. Focusing her attention on Lidia, she lost her smile. "Good day," she said and went back to checking in a short stack of books.

Walking out into a parking lot surrounded by thick, beautiful trees, Nikki turned back and examined the cozy yellow house. "This house belonged to Mr. and Mrs. Sheffield. In 1984, the town converted it into the library," Lidia explained, ready to pinch Nikki's neck off. "Did you see the look she gave me? Cold as ice."

"Well, she was smiling...at first," Nikki tried to comfort her friend. "I guess a light went off in her attic. I'll drive you back to the store."

Standing in a refreshing breeze that smelled of roses, Lidia shook her head no. "Listen, Nikki, you're a sweet woman, and I'm glad we're friends. But my husband and I live simple lives. We like our life here in Maple Hills. People know me, and I know them. I can't afford to become a black sheep, okay? I'll see you at the store tomorrow...that is, if I still have a job."

"Of course, you do," Nikki promised Lidia and gave her a grateful hug. "And you have my word, from this point forward, I'm a solo woman. I hereby take the handcuffs off you."

Appreciating Nikki's humor, Lidia allowed herself to relax. So what if Mrs. Slokam gave her a cold eye; who cared? If people asked, she would simply tell those nosy do-gooders that she was helping a friend do research. And if she was really pressed, she would hold her ground and stubbornly proclaim that she helped the newcomer in town because the lady happened to be her boss, and she needed a job. "I'll walk back to the store; it's only a few blocks from here. And to be honest, I could use the walk."

"Okay," Nikki told Lidia. "I'll see you tomorrow morning."

Nikki walked to her white SUV and crawled in. From instinct, she guessed Chief Daily was going to pay the library a visit anyway. Hanging around and having her cell phone checked was not an option. Throwing the SUV into reverse, she got moving. Minutes later, a chubby man with thick gray hair pulled into the parking lot and parked a brown and white patrol car in the same spot Nikki had been parked.

5

Hearing the tea kettle begin to cry and whine, Nikki walked to the stove with her cell phone in hand. Scrolling through the photos she had taken of the newspapers back at the library, it seemed to her that each person written about had been a specific target. Clicking off the stove, Nikki grabbed an oven mitt hanging over her head from the wooden pot rack. Picking up the tea kettle, with her eyes examining the photos, she poured water into a cream-colored mug. "I would like to speak with each of these people, but I wouldn't guess they would lay out a welcome mat for me. I'd most likely get a few doors slammed in my face and a few complaints filed against me...which would harm my store."

Pondering her options as she set the tea kettle back on the stove, Nikki decided that the best path for her to follow, for the time being, was a path that allowed her to simply play dumb. After all, the only real person she had to deal with was probably Chief Daily—that was, if he even opted to pay her a visit. With the newspapers properly secured, Chief Daily would most likely keep Nikki's sudden burst of curiosity on the back burner and get around to her in a manner associated with police work instead of personal interest. "A man is dead, and I go snooping around sensitive papers...not smart," Nikki scolded herself, dropping a blackberry tea bag into her mug. "But what choice did I have? The killer—or killers—might have paid a visit to the library and disposed of the papers. I had to see the paper and act fast, but still, gotta be more careful in the future."

Deciding to get some fresh air, Nikki walked to the duck pond. Sitting down on a wooden bench near the pond, she drew in a breath of lovely, fresh air. Tall, gorgeous trees hugged the backyard, creating absolute privacy. Healthy and bright flower gardens circled the pond, ending up at the wooden bench Nikki was sitting on. A river rock walking path stood between the flower gardens and the pond. To Nikki, her backyard was a dream come true. So beautiful, so serene, so tranquil, so... Hearing her cell phone ring, she felt her inner peace shatter. "Well," she told the four ducks living in the pond, all of them lazily floating on the water with bored, gray eyes, "it was nice while it lasted."

Setting the mug down on the bench, Nikki examined the incoming number. Recognizing the call as a local number, she hit the accept button. "Hello, Nikki Bates speaking," she said, forcing her voice to sound friendly and nice.

"Get out of town or else," a cruel, harsh voice hissed at Nikki.

"Why would I do that?" Nikki asked, feeling fear grip her chest. Through years of experience, she had learned never to show fear, even though fear had become one of her greatest enemies. Standing up from the bench, she began to study the tree line for any sign of movement.

"Get out of town or else," the voice hissed again, and the call ended.

Drawing in a deep breath, Nikki lowered the cell phone from her ear. She kept patrolling the tree line with her eyes. Even though it seemed like Maple Hills was a safe haven compared to Atlanta, Nikki clearly realized as she examined her backyard that danger could swallow her whole in a small town just as quickly as it could in a metropolis. If the caller was lurking out in the woods, hiding behind a tree, watching her, holding a gun—or worse, aiming a rifle at her—she couldn't tell. The wonderful, thick, beautiful nature she adored had now become a strange and dangerous curtain that hid potential threats from her view.

Unable to control the tightness in her chest, Nikki picked up her mug and jogged back to the house, glancing over her shoulder a few times. With the kitchen door securely locked behind her, she sat down at the kitchen table. "I can't become a prisoner in my own home," she said in a shaky voice. "Come on, Bates, you've gotten worse calls than that back home. Now think...the caller was a man. Age? No age, he was muffling his voice...local number...caller knows I was at the library snooping around."

Deciding to jump onto the internet and investigate the

number, Nikki hurried into the living room where her laptop sat on a pine desk. She pulled back her computer chair and sat down.

"Okay, white pages will do," she said, placing her cell phone down onto the desk and hopping onto the internet. "Let's see what we get..." Going to the white pages website, Nikki went to the reverse phone option and typed in the number belonging to the caller. "The hospital...Dr. Ronald Mayton, did you give me a call?"

The thought of a bitter, hateful old doctor trying to scare Nikki made her feel better, somewhat. Yes, the threatening call had come from the hospital, but it wasn't clear who. However, if Ronald Mayton had placed the call, it raised two questions: First, how did he get Nikki's cell phone number, and second, how did he know she was at the library snooping around? "I filled out a form when I applied for my library card," Nikki told herself, "and I wrote down my cell phone number. Seems like Mrs. Slokam is a little trickier than I thought."

Tapping her fingertips against the desk, Nikki struggled to decide if she should report the call to Chief Daily or pay the hospital a personal visit. "My address is on the library form," she reminded herself. "Better go pay the hospital a visit. Perhaps if I confront this Ronald Mayton character, he'll back down."

Sitting still a minute longer, Nikki carefully evaluated her options. She had a call that had come from the hospital recorded on her cell phone. That fact was to her advantage. But she didn't have proof Ronald Mayton had placed the call and threatened her. If she went barging into the hospital making accusations that could not be backed up with solid proof, she was liable to accomplish nothing more than having the police chase her away. Being the new woman in town—a new woman who was running her very own business—the last thing Nikki wanted was to create a division between her and the people she wanted to call her new neighbors. Rubbing people the wrong way, especially people on the city council, might cause her business license to suddenly be revoked, her property taxes to soar, or a suspicious visit from a building inspector who would surely find something wrong with her cabin and insist she fix the fabricated problems, which would surely cost more money than she had. Oh yes, there were ways of running people out of town, and if she didn't play nice, Nikki knew she would become a prime target.

"That's the ticket," she said, smiling. "Why, I've got a desperate migraine. I need to pay a visit to the ER. Perhaps the on-call physician can assist me with my problem."

Standing up from her desk, Nikki closed the laptop, ran into the kitchen, grabbed her purse, and took off. Feeling the old excitement that once consumed her mind back in Atlanta, she felt alive and energized, passionate and determined. Speeding off in her SUV, she felt like a woman on fire. If she were forced out of town with what money there was in her savings, Nikki knew she would barely have enough to buy a one-bedroom house back home. She had invested all of her money into her new home, new business, and new life, leaving only a small nest-egg sitting in her savings account.

Stopping at a four-way stop sign, Nikki suddenly felt all

her energy drain from her body. What was she doing? What was she really doing? Stirring up a hornets' nest, was what. Yet, she had to protect herself. A man was dead. She was new in town. The man had come into her store. The man owned a newspaper. She'd worked for a major newspaper in Atlanta. Questions would be asked—questions that might make the people of Maple Hills decide to transform Nikki Bates into the perfect scapegoat. If the killer was a local, Nikki was finished.

Allowing her eyes to rest on the beauty of the serene streets, Nikki thought about the old German couple. "Denforth looked straight at them and then left the store," she whispered. "Whoever killed him might know about the poisonous stories he published...and might use that to cover up the killing, causing suspicion to be cast to the right instead of the left."

Letting up off the brake, Nikki eased her SUV through the stop sign and drove to the small, one-story brick hospital sitting on a hill, looking down at the town like a broken-down old machine barely capable of producing a simple puff of smoke, let alone function with efficient skill. Parking in the emergency room parking area, which was basically just the left side of the visitors' parking lot, she exited the SUV and casually glanced around. As far as she could see, business was bad for the ER. Only her SUV and two other vehicles sat parked in the ER area, and the rest of the parking lot was empty. That's when a strange thought rolled into her mind like a heavy whisper of fog. "Mrs. Slokam called Chief Daily and reported me snooping around the newspapers. Surely he would have been too tied up with the murder to take her call? And this parking lot is practically deserted. If Denforth's body had been brought here, where are the reporters? Where are the law enforcement officials? Something smells rotten in Denmark."

6

Walking up to the emergency room entrance, Nikki struggled to put together the pieces of the puzzle she had. She entered a fancy waiting area demarcated with beautiful art, exquisite chairs, lovely potted plants, soft blue painted walls, and a spotless white marble floor. "It's gorgeous," she whispered, clearly taken aback by the expense before her.

Looking around the waiting room, Nikki didn't see a single person. Spotting an old woman sitting at a wooden desk that cost more than she would make in a lifetime, she shrugged her shoulders. "Has to be the check-in desk."

The desk sat in a corner like a comfortable old shoe; Nikki forced a painful smile on her face and approached it. "Excuse me, but is this where I need to check in? You see, my migraine is back..."

The old woman, who appeared to be older than time itself, looked up from a novel she was reading. "No, dear, you go through that door right there, and you'll see the check-in area to your left. I'm just here to greet people."

"Oh," Nikki said, confused, feeling as if she were in a fancy hotel instead of a hospital, "okay. Thank you. Uh...if it's all right to ask, can you tell me what doctor is on call?"

"Dr. Mayton," the old woman smiled sweetly at Nikki. "I'm sure he'll be able to help you with your migraine. I used to get them all the time myself. Dr. Mayton will be able to help you."

"Through that door?" Nikki pointed to a wooden door.

"Through that door," the old woman told Nikki.

Nikki walked off and then paused. Looking over her shoulder, she saw the old woman go back to reading her novel. "What's going on here?" she whispered. "But first things first, let's pay Dr. Mayton a visit."

Opening the wooden door, Nikki stepped into a short, gray-carpeted hallway that smelled like a combination of roses and pine needles. On her left stood two cubicles. Each cubicle held a single, plain-looking, wooden desk with a computer. Two simple gray chairs sat on each side of the desk. It was obvious the waiting room was for show, to impress the tourists, should one need emergency assistance. "Hello?" Nikki called out, finding both cubicles empty. Spotting an open door behind the cubicles, Nikki narrowed her eyes and looked into a room that appeared to be designed for coffee breaks. "Hello?" she called out again.

"Yes?" a woman asked, walking out of the room holding a can of soda in her hand.

Nikki forced a polite smile. "Yes, I am here because my migraine headache has become something fierce," she explained, studying the woman with the soda can. The woman was her age, tall, skinnier than a toothpick, and she had stringy blond hair that was obviously dyed. Between the woman's hair and the ugly, short and tight dress she was wearing, Nikki wasn't sure if she was on planet earth anymore. Why did women her age insist on dressing like teenagers? Didn't the woman realize that she looked like a goofy scarecrow?

"Take a seat," the woman told Nikki, obviously annoyed that she was going to have to work instead of wasting the hospital's money standing around in the break room and hoping Prince Charming would swoop in and rescue her from her dreary life.

"I'll take her," another woman said, walking out of the break room. This woman, Nikki saw, was her own age, too, but had some form of common sense. The woman had an average build with short black hair and a pretty face, much prettier than the scarecrow woman. And unlike the scarecrow woman, she was dressed modestly, wearing a long tan dress with elbow-length sleeves. "Hi, my name is Jane Milsap...no kin to Ronnie Milsap," she joked, sitting down after the scarecrow woman wandered back into the break room. "How can I help you today?"

Relieved to be speaking with someone pleasant, Nikki explained about her fake migraine. But then something told her Jane saw right through her lies. "I believe Dr. Mayton is on duty?"

"He is," Jane said, placing her hands down onto the computer keyboard. "Okay, let's get started. Name, please."

Nikki painfully went through the check-in process,

ending by surrendering her insurance card for Jane to photocopy. "Thank you," Nikki said, taking back her insurance card. "Should I go wait in the waiting room?"

"Oh no," Jane offered Nikki a friendly smile, "I'm sure we can make room for you in the back."

"It is kinda slow," Nikki agreed and then decided to toss some bait at Jane to see if the woman would take a nibble. "I wasn't sure if I could be seen today. I heard that a poor man was run over in town."

Jane bit down on her lower lip. Cautiously, she shifted through the papers she had printed out for Nikki to sign and then placed her hands together. Jane saw her wedding band. "Mrs.—"

"I'm divorced," Nikki quickly interrupted.

"I'm sorry," Jane said in a sincere and compassionate voice. "Ms. Bates, I'm aware of who you are. You opened the new store downtown, Chocolate Covered Delights. This is a small town; newcomers are quickly investigated and gossiped about."

Nikki smiled. A woman like Jane was obviously intelligent—a woman she could respect and come to like as a friend. "You know I moved here from Atlanta, then?"

"And I know you worked for a very prominent newspaper there, too," Jane explained. "Word around town is that you were over at the library earlier, too?"

"Wow, word travels fast in a small town," Nikki said, clearly allowing Jane to lead the conversation. "Yes, I was at the library earlier."

"You realize the man who was killed this morning caused the citizens of this fair town quite some distress? I'm sorry to say that his death is a cause for celebration rather than grief."

Understanding the hint Jane was tossing into her lap and appreciating the kindness, Nikki stood up. "Perhaps I can see Dr. Mayton now?"

"This is a small town," Jane said, standing up with Nikki. "This isn't Atlanta. Whatever your hound dog nose has a scent of, please drop it. But I can tell by looking into your eyes that you won't, which leaves me with one other choice..."

"Which is?" Nikki asked, preparing for the worst.

"Tonight, seven o'clock, my home. I'm inviting you to have dinner with my husband and me. I hope you like spaghetti."

Seeing honesty in Jane's eyes—the same honesty she saw in Lidia—comforted Nikki's nerves. "Are you sure you want to be seen with a trouble maker?"

"I was a trouble maker once myself," Jane winked at Nikki. "Follow me."

7

Dr. Ronald Mayton pulled back a privacy curtain, stared at Nikki, and then yanked the curtain closed behind him. "My nurse tells me you are suffering from migraines?" he asked in a cold tone.

Unreal, Nikki thought, casting her eyes on the short, plump man with thin, grayish-black hair. He looks like an unemployed plumber wearing a bad suit. "Yes, my migraine began right after I received a very disturbing call," Nikki answered. Sitting on a gurney covered with a sheet, she slowly eased her way down onto the clean floor. The small, curtained room held a simple blood pressure machine and a red box attached to the back wall for discarded needles.

"I see," Dr. Mayton replied, narrowing his eyes at Nikki. Shoving his hands down into the white lab coat he was wearing over his cheap gray suit, he grew silent for a minute. "You know it was me, then? Otherwise, why would you be here?"

"I checked the number on white pages. It would have been smarter to use an outside number," Nikki agreed patiently. "Why did you threaten me?"

"Listen," Dr. Mayton snapped in a low growl, "Denforth already smeared my name in the press once. I don't need a hot-shot reporter from Atlanta doing it again. Yeah, word around town is that you're digging into the murder to get a hot story, to make a name for yourself around here."

So that's what people are thinking. Here I am trying to protect myself, and people around this town think I'm after a story, Nikki thought. Kicking herself for being overly paranoid and believing that suspicion would fall onto her, she shook her head. Small town naivety destroys big city gut instincts. "I could report you to the police."

"My word against yours," Dr. Mayton told Nikki. "I can deny any claims made against me."

"Maybe," Nikki agreed, "but I have the power of the press. I can call my old editor in Atlanta and have him spread your name all across the front page."

All the color drained out of Dr. Mayton's face. Sure, he had called and threatened Nikki, but a phone call was as far as he was willing to go. Jail time awaited him if he ever laid a violent hand on a woman again; the judge in Boston had made that point extremely clear to him. "What do you want...money? Did you come here to blackmail me?"

"I want information," Nikki insisted. "Why did Denforth write about you in the paper? Did you know him?"

"Did I know him?" Dr. Mayton asked in a disgusted voice. "Nobody knew this guy. He shows up out of nowhere and starts writing garbage about people. He knew about my life in Boston. And then..."

"And then what?" Nikki pressed.

"The blackmail began. Denforth, that rotten skunk, began demanding money from the people he wrote about, or else he would send the stories he wrote to larger papers. Come on lady, you're a reporter, you must know everyone he wrote about has money," Dr. Mayton hissed.

Nikki rubbed the back of her neck with her hand. Up until now, she had not put those clues together. "Do you believe a local, someone Denforth wrote about, killed him?"

"No way," Dr. Mayton said, shaking his head. "Why take the chance? We paid him the blackmail money. But whoever ran him down did me a huge favor. Good riddance to that sewer rat."

"Will the others Denforth wrote about speak with me?"

"Definitely not," Dr. Mayton clearly informed Nikki in a tone that told her that trying to interview anyone else would result in disaster. "And now that Denforth is dead, we can finally leave town. He kept us here under the power of blackmail, but now we're free. So if you think for one minute I'm going to pay you—"

"I don't want your money," Nikki told Dr. Mayton, "I'm an honest reporter. But rest assured if you ever call me again in the manner you did earlier, I will report you to every authority known to mankind. And by the way, my cell phone has recorded this entire conversation. So you're the one who'd better be leaving Maple Hills."

"Lady," Dr. Mayton promised, "I can't get out of this sewer fast enough. Are you through?"

"One more question?"

"Last one," Dr. Mayton answered, annoyed.

"Was Denforth working alone?"

"How should I know? Every month I mailed my money to a post office box in Boston," Dr. Mayton snapped. "Now listen, I can't leave town immediately. If I do, well, I might look suspicious. But I'm leaving as soon as I can. Is that good enough for you?"

"Yes," Nikki agreed, "but before I go, I do have one last question."

"No more questions—"

"Denforth had more on you, didn't he? By the way, you try and hide your Brooklyn accent, my guess is you are or were connected with the mob. You have that look," Nikki told Dr. Mayton examining every feature of his face. "You have that talk."

"Oh, gee, lady," Dr. Mayton said, feeling the color drain from his face again. "I was..." Dr. Mayton lowered his voice to a whisper, "that was a long time ago. I was a stupid kid, okay? That was way back."

Nikki studied Dr. Mayton's face. "You stole money, left town, went to medical school, started a new life, and here you are, right? Somehow Denforth found out."

"That rat found out a lot about a lot of people," Dr. Mayton told Nikki, narrowing his eyes at her. "Yeah, I'm not perfect, and maybe what that rat wrote about me is true, but I got out, you hear me? I got out before I got killed. Like I said, I was just a stupid nineteen-year-old kid who didn't have any sense to know better."

"I have no more interest in you. But rest assured this

conversation is going to be safeguarded. If you try to harm me, it'll go straight to the police," Nikki said, pointing to her cell phone.

"Yeah, yeah," Dr. Mayton said, throwing his hands in the air, "take a hike. I'm not going to prison over some lame-brain reporter who can't keep her nose clean. Get lost."

8

Confident she had picked all the information Dr. Mayton was willing to surrender, Nikki walked out of the curtained room. As she did, she bumped right into Chief Daily. "How is your migraine, Ms. Bates?" he asked in an angry tone.

Going with the idea that everyone thought she was a reporter after a hot story, Nikki shrugged her shoulders. Having a card up her sleeve might just be the ticket she needed to keep the wolves who might want to begin nipping at her ankle at bay. Blackmail through the press was a powerful tool. "It comes and goes. Chief Daily, I presume?"

Dr. Mayton stuck his head out of the curtain, eyed Chief Daily with a nervous face, and scurried away like the rat he was. "This way," Chief Daily ordered Nikki, leading her back out into the fancy waiting room. Nikki followed behind Chief Daily, wondering why the man was wearing an expensive suit that, from what she could see, cost well into the thousands. Why wasn't Chief Daily wearing his police uniform? "I see you had a little talk with our beloved doctor?"

Standing close to the sliding glass doors, Nikki watched the old woman who had greeted her stand up and vanish through the door leading into the check-in area. All alone. "Awful quiet around here," she replied, ignoring the question. "A man was murdered, but you couldn't tell it. This silence in this place is so loud it could pop your eardrums."

"The body of the hit-and-run victim has been transferred to the state capital. Our medical facility isn't equipped to—"

"This hospital doesn't have a morgue?" Nikki interrupted, throwing her arms together. She'd gone toe-to-toe with plenty of police officials in her past. The jerk standing before her wasn't someone she was prepared to back down from. "Oh come on, Chief, I've been fed better lines by street dealers trying to sell me stolen watches." Nikki felt the blood of the sleeping reporter in her begin to boil.

"Listen, the body was transferred to the morgue in Montpelier."

"Mighty quick," Nikki said. Before she could say another word, the sliding glass doors opened. A tall, handsome man with short blond hair walked in. He wore an open-collared blue button-up shirt over a white t-shirt, tucked into a pair of jeans. The man, Nikki guessed, was about her age.

"You must be the thorn in my pop's side," the man told Nikki. Extending his hand, he introduced himself. "My name is Hawk Daily. And before you ask, yes, my first name is really Hawk. My pop was once a hippie."

"I couldn't tell," Nikki said in a sarcastic tone, casting a hard eye at Chief Daily while she shook Hawk Daily's hand. "Maybe you can tell me why the body of the hit-and-run victim was rushed out of town?"

"I was wondering that myself," Hawk answered honestly. "The guy eats the front of an SUV and the next thing we know the Germans are ordering his body removed from town."

"The Germans?" Nikki exclaimed. In her mind, she saw the old German couple in her store.

"Yeah, really shook Pop up. That's why he's wearing his fancy suit," Hawk explained. "Some big shot from Washington is supposed to be paying us a visit in the next few hours."

"Listen, big mouth, if you like your job as a detective, keep your mouth shut," Chief Daily snapped at Hawk.

"Detective," Nikki said, impressed. "What do you investigate in Maple Hills? Who sneaks around in the middle of the night raising the flags on mailboxes?"

"You have a sense of humor, I like that," Hawk smiled at Nikki. "Beautiful, witty, and a real pain in my pop's butt. Will you marry me?"

Instead of tossing a witty comeback at Hawk, Nikki blushed. "I..."

"My son worked for the NYPD. He retired three years ago. I hired him as the Senior Detective. His experience qualifies him, so if you—"

"It's okay, Chief Daily," Nikki interrupted, feeling Hawk

absorb her beauty into his eyes, "I have no doubt your son is fully qualified for the position he holds." Steadying herself, Nikki pushed herself out of the halls of high school and returned to adulthood. Looking Hawk in the eye, she pressed: "Any idea why the Germans wanted the body?"

Hawk shrugged his shoulders. "The deceased didn't have any identification on him. After I ran his fingerprints, *bam*! Next thing I know the FBI is calling me. Some joker named Agent Ferguson claiming the man who had eaten a concrete dinner was being sought by the Germans."

"You go writing this, and I'll throw you in jail," Chief Daily threatened Nikki. "Look, you seem like a nice woman, and we here in Maple Hills are happy to have you as a part of our community. We're a quiet community, though, a community that respects its people. The deceased, as you know by now, wrote many horrible lies about some of the most upstanding members of our town. That man is dead now. We will heal from his lies and put this whole ugly mess behind us."

"Nice speech," Nikki slipped before she could catch her mouth. "I'm sorry. I do understand. I began my own investigation because I feared suspicion of Denforth's murder might be cast on me. I am new in town. Denforth and I both worked for major newspapers. And Denforth was in my store that morning. After he left, he got run down."

Hawk scratched the back of his head. "I can see why you were worried, but you were in your store when Denforth was creamed. I already spoke to your employees. You're in the clear."

"Am I?" Nikki asked. "Suppose the murderer is a local? He or she could try to frame me for the murder."

"Possibly," Hawk agreed, understanding Nikki's concern. "But I don't think this was a local job. The description of the SUV doesn't match up."

"The SUV had no tag," Nikki pointed out.

"Yes, but no vehicle in Maple Hills fits that description," Hawk explained. "My bet? This was a professional hit. Here we are flooded with tourists, hundreds of out-of-state tags, and out of nowhere explodes this black SUV with tinted windows that runs Denforth down. Now, Maple Hills does have quite a few black SUVs, but not a single one of them has tinted windows. Dark tinted windows—"

"I know," Nikki sighed. "Listen, Detective Daily—"

"Call me Hawk."

"Okay, Hawk," Nikki smiled, suddenly feeling exhausted. "Earlier Dr. Mayton called my cell phone and told me to leave town. I traced the call back to this hospital. We had a chat. He was afraid I might smear his name again. Long story short, as soon as he can leave town without it seeming suspicious, well, he's outta here."

Hawk rubbed his chin. "I never liked that weasel. Good riddance to him."

"I agree," Nikki supported Hawk's statement, "but the fact of the matter is, he won't be the only one leaving. Listen, I'm suddenly feeling emotionally tapped out. Why don't you come over to my store tomorrow morning around nine? We'll have coffee and talk some more."

"How about dinner tonight?" Hawk asked, giving Nikki his most charming smile.

"I can't. I'm having dinner with a friend," Nikki apologized. "My husband and I also divorced...the divorce was messy. Hawk, thank you for the offer, but right now—"

"You need a friend," Hawk finished, nodding his head. "Hey, you want a friend, I can be a friend," he said and tipped Nikki a friendly smile. "My ex-wife didn't exactly say goodbye to me with her claws tucked into her paws. It took me some time, too. I completely understand."

"Thank you," Nikki said gratefully. "Before I go, I want to remind you that everyone Denforth wrote about could be the person who ran him down. I learned that each person seems to have lots of money. Perhaps they didn't kill Denforth, but they could have hired someone. I would contact each person directly and tell them to remain in town, including Dr. Mayton and Mr. Hyde."

Chief Daily let out a loud groan. "Yeah, all right. Hawk, you start making the calls. I'll go tell Mayton to hang around."

"I'll speak with Mayton," Hawk said and tipped Nikki another wink. "See you tomorrow morning for coffee." Hawk started for the door leading into the check-in area and then paused. Turning around, he focused on Nikki. "You said Denforth was in your store. Did he buy anything? Did he speak to anyone? Was he with anyone?"

Nikki shook her head no. "I was at the register dealing with a customer when I heard the bells over the front door ring. I saw Denforth walk in, look around, and then leave."

"Could be he was searching for someone?" Hawk suggested.

"Yes, it could have been," Nikki agreed, keeping the

information about the old German couple secret. "Well, I need to go to my store and check on a few items. I'll see you tomorrow morning."

"Wait a minute," Chief Daily growled, "let me remind you that if you write one word about Denforth—even on the back of a piece of toilet paper—I'll have you behind bars quicker than you can say 'uh oh.' Am I making myself clear, Ms. Bates? This case is extremely confidential and very sensitive."

"In other words, Pop doesn't want the FBI breathing down his neck because you busted this case open to the mainstream press," Hawk rolled his eyes. "Pop doesn't like the Feds. For some reason, the Feds make him nervous."

"I just don't like having Washington looking into my corner of the world," Chief Daily exploded at his son. "Maple Hills is a—"

"Yeah, I know," Hawk said, rolling his eyes again, "Maple Hills is a quiet community where the upstanding members sit around holding hands and watching *Mr. Rogers' Neighborhood* all day and forget that every word Denforth wrote about them was backed up with hard evidence."

Nikki watched Hawk walk away, leaving Chief Daily fuming. Shrugging her shoulders, she excused herself and walked outside. "Day one...very interesting," she said, walking to her SUV. "I can't wait to see what day two brings."

9

Startled, Nikki slowly closed the front door to her cabin. The old German couple who had visited her store stood in front of the fireplace, staring at her with calm, blue eyes. "How can I help you?" Nikki asked, forcing her voice to sound brave instead of alarmed. Dinner with Jane and her husband had been nice. Making new friends was always welcome. Coming home to strangers in her living room was not.

"You are Nikki Bates, yes?" the old woman asked.

"Yes," Nikki agreed, hanging her purse on a wooden coat rack standing next to the front door. Usually, she would take her purse into the kitchen out of habit, but just in case she needed to make a hasty escape, she wanted her purse where she could reach it fast. "I'm Nikki Bates."

The old woman glanced at the old man standing next to her. "My name is Adal Hochberg, and this is my husband, Johan."

Nikki noticed that Adal was wearing a dark gray dress

that went all the way down to her feet, and Johan was wearing a dark gray suit. Their appearance immediately told Nikki what she had been secretly thinking. "I am sorry about your son. I know you must be very upset. Please, sit down."

"We will stand," Johan said in his thick German accent, much thicker than that of his wife. "We have come to ask for your assistance."

"Please," Nikki held out her hand to the couch, "sit down. You both look tired." Guessing that Adal and Johan had to be at least in their late seventies, Nikki felt compassion for them. Sure, she knew, people who have aged in years were still as dangerous as young street thugs, but the two elderly people standing in her living room were not dangerous.

Adal nodded her head. "Yes, it has been a very tiring day. Johan, sit with me."

Nikki watched Johan as he walked his wife to the couch, helped her sit down, and then—reluctantly—sat down himself. "How did you know the man killed today was our son?" he asked with eyes formed from years of brilliant thinking.

"Your son came into my store, spotted you and your wife standing at the counter, and left. When I was informed that his body was taken to the state morgue at the request of the German government, I just kinda put two and two together," Nikki explained, walking to the fireplace to face Adal and Johan.

"Our son...he was no good," Adal confessed miserably. "Brilliant, clever, witty...charming...but vicious as a poison spider and heartless as a scorpion. But he was our son, and we grieve for a life that was lived in darkness."

"We spent a fortune tracking our son. We almost caught him in New York, but he escaped," Johan explained, patting his wife's hand. "Our son was part of the German Mafia, I'm afraid. He escaped from New York without a trace, which made it very difficult for our people to continue searching for him."

"What is his real name?" Nikki asked.

"Hanz Hochberg," Adal confessed. "Ms. Bates, our son knew how to manipulate his environments to succeed in his criminal work. We are aware of the trouble he caused certain citizens of this town by publishing damaging facts about them in the local paper. That is like our Hanz...he was always a bully, but with his mind, not his hands."

"Seems to me like he knew exactly how to manipulate Maple Hills," Nikki agreed. "He comes here to hide, starts investigating the people, comes up with some dirt, uses the paper as his muscle, and starts blackmailing people for money. And I'm guessing he never worked for the paper in New York—that was all a lie, a lie to threaten people with." Nikki thought about Dr. Mayton.

"A criminal mind is like fire, never satisfied and always hungry and very clever at lies," Johan explained. "Our son was considered a genius. We had such high hopes for his future. Perhaps in medicine, like myself."

"At a young age, he became involved in crime," Adal continued, "and soon the German Mafia consumed his soul. They used his mind, his brilliant mind, as a dangerous weapon. Our son cherished the excitement, the danger, the money..."

"Hanz Hochberg was the mastermind behind a series of bank robberies which, in U.S. currency, amounted to two hundred eighty-four million dollars. Eight people were murdered during the robberies," Johan explained.

Nikki whistled to herself. "Two hundred and eighty-four million dollars."

"Over the course of ten years," Johan pointed out. "Before the German authorities could arrest him, he fled to America."

"Our son had a weakness," Adal told Nikki, "a woman named Fredricka Kraus." Adal paused as if a horrible taste had entered her mouth. "This woman, too, was no good. She had an empty soul, incapable of loving anyone but herself. When my son contacted her, she immediately went to the German Authorities hoping to obtain reward money."

"I see," Nikki said, "she betrayed Hanz."

Johan shook his head. "When he fled New York, we were informed he fled with an amount of money that to you and me would be quite substantial...but to Hanz, mere pennies. Hanz always hungered for more and more money. Money equaled power to him."

"Hiding in a small town surely wouldn't be easy for a man like him..." Nikki said in a low voice, slowly putting Hanz Hochberg together in her mind. The man killed was no ordinary criminal. "How did you locate your son here in Maple Hills?" she asked.

"The fire," Johan told Nikki, exhausted. Shifting on the couch to find a more comfortable position he drew quietly into his own thoughts for a few minutes. "The building that housed the newspaper was burned down by our son."

"How do you know that?" Nikki asked.

"There is an arsonist in Germany who is spending the rest of his life in prison. This man knew my son. They both were in the German Mafia together. We saw this man many times with our son. They were, as you say here in America...pals," Adal explained in a sad tone. "But what could my husband and I do? The German Mafia...their power reaches everywhere. We attempted to save our son by every means—"

"You don't have to explain anything to me," Nikki assured Adal, reading the misery in her eyes. "I've seen kids at the age of ten eaten alive by street gangs. I understand. Now, about this arsonist?"

"The style in which the newspaper building was destroyed matched the style of the arsonist rotting in prison back in Germany," Johan told Nikki. "Our private investigators came across the story about the fire. We paid them to remain silent and not inform the German authorities. We wanted to locate Hanz ourselves, plead with him to return to Germany. Even in prison, our son would be alive. Can you understand, Ms. Bates?"

"Yes. I have a son of my own," Nikki replied. Taking a deep breath, she began to wonder why Hanz remained in town after burning down the newspaper building. "Mr. and Mrs. Hochberg, why would Hanz have remained in Maple Hills after the fire? For that matter, how did he even choose Maple Hills, unless..."

Adal closed her eyes. "You are a very smart woman. Yes,

what you are thinking is true. Hanz knew a woman in this village. We made inquiries, found out the name our son was hiding beneath, had our investigators search the company that provides internet service to your village along with all calls made by cell phones in this location."

"As well as the mail," Johan continued. "It seems our son was saving the money mailed to a post office box in Boston. Our investigators took photos of a woman retrieving the money. After taking her fingerprints off the post office box, they researched her identity."

"Impressive," Nikki said, walking to one of her sitting chairs. "Mind if I sit down?"

"Please," Adal urged Nikki. "We were given the woman's address. We watched the woman carefully but never once saw our son. We did see her husband," Adal finished, feeling ashamed.

"The time came to flush out our son, so we approached the woman and pressured her," Johan told Nikki, watching her sit down. "We gave her no other choice but to assist us. Either she helped us, or we would have words with her husband."

"The woman agreed to help us. She went to our son and set up a meeting. We were supposed to meet in this town," Adal told Nikki.

"In my store," Nikki said, feeling her shoulders begin to ache.

"Yes," Adal nodded.

"Who is this woman?" Nikki gently pressed, having a sudden craving for hot coffee and chocolate.

"A woman by the name of Wendy Phillips, an employee

at the newspaper my son purchased," Johan informed Nikki.

Nikki felt her mind connect a few dots. "And I bet this Wendy Phillips helped your son dig up the dirt he used to blackmail the people he wrote about. I bet she even wrote the stories herself."

"This woman claims she loved our son. Her husband, he is abusive, yes," Adal said, weakly defending the woman. "After the fire, she claimed our son remained in town because he loved her. I am not so certain, but why else would he have remained?"

"Perhaps she was blackmailing him, yes?" Johan suggested.

"Why are you speaking with me about this?" Nikki asked. Outside in the night, she heard the winds begin to pick up. "I'm assuming the matter is not over if you are here?"

"Our son was murdered by someone in this village. My husband and I wish for you to locate the killer. We wish to return to Germany with peaceful minds. Today we heard gossip about you. We had you researched. The results of our research appealed to us," Adal told Nikki, slowly standing up. "I need to stand," she told her husband.

"You are in a position to help us. The local authorities are of no use to us," Johan explained, watching his wife walk to the fireplace. "We will pay you very nicely."

"I don't want your money," Nikki told Johan, now hearing the wind begin to howl outside. A storm was approaching. "I'll help you because you deserve the peace you hunger for. I'll also help you because if what you say is true, then there is a killer loose in this town." Standing up, Nikki studied the front door. "It's going to be storming soon. Please, remain here tonight. You can sleep in my guest room. Tomorrow we will talk more."

Adal nodded her head at her husband. "Yes, I am tired, Johan. We need to rest."

Johan agreed.

Later, after the Hochbergs were asleep, Nikki went into the kitchen and made a fresh pot of coffee. While the coffee was brewing, she pulled some ingredients out of the cabinets and listened to a heavy rain falling outside. She had a long night of thinking ahead of her, and she thought best when she made chocolate and drank coffee. "Well," she said, taking down a bag of chocolate chips, "my next step is to find the killer. But who? Wendy Phillips' husband? One of the people Hanz wrote about? Wendy Phillips herself? Someone killed Hanz Hochberg, and I have to find out who."

Pausing with the bag of chocolate chips in her hands, Nikki thought about Hanz Hochberg. She thought about the brief seconds her eyes had held the man in her sight. The mere sight of him would have never revealed the dark shadows lurking beneath his skin. "And it all ended for him in a small town in Vermont," Nikki said, shaking her head. "But the question now is...who ended it?"

10

Nikki wasn't surprised to find the guest room empty and the Hochbergs gone when she woke up. She half laughed to herself. "They'll be in touch," she said, taking a sip of coffee. "In the meantime, I better get dressed. I have to meet Hawk at nine, but I need a shower first."

After taking a hot shower, Nikki threw on a dress, tossed her hair into a pony-tail and hurried out the front door, grabbing her purse the way an outfielder would snag a foul ball. Small-town living was supposed to be peaceful, but Nikki felt like she was back in Atlanta as she jogged to her SUV, parked in the driveway next to the cabin. Jogging across wet grass, taking in deep breaths of damp, clean air, she thought back to all the jogging she did in her hometown, how peaceful those mornings had been. A strong feeling of homesickness struck her heart. "Not now," she said, unlocking the SUV and jumping into the driver's seat.

Backing down the driveway, Nikki put her mind to work. "What do we have so far?" Nikki asked herself, driving down the quiet back-country road leading into town. "We have Hanz Hochberg, alias Steven Denforth. The man is from Germany, tied to the German Mafia, comes to America, ends up in Maple Hills because he needed a place to hide and somehow knew Wendy Phillips. Hanz's parents are able to track him down. They strong-arm Phillips to set up a meeting with their son. On the same day the meeting was to take place, Hanz is killed. By whom? There's a long list of suspects..."

Entering Maple Hills, Nikki drove through sleepy neighborhoods lined with quaint, gingerbread-like homes on one street and fancy two-story homes with neatly trimmed lawns on another street. Maple Hills did not have any poor neighborhoods or trailer parks. Most tourist towns didn't. The streets Nikki eased through were quiet, clean, cozy—no rundown houses, no cars blaring loud music, no litter lining the sidewalks, no graffiti. *But hidden in this town, behind all of the pretty homes, lie the same crimes, just presented in a different package*, she reflected.

Leaving the residential area, Nikki drove by sleeping little shops that would soon be filled with rich tourists. There was a candle shop, an antique store, a collectible bookstore, and a shop selling honey, jams, and bread. The stores nestled in buildings that looked as though they had arrived straight from Switzerland. Swinging the SUV into a parking spot right in front of her shop, Nikki eased her eyes to the left and right. It was 8:45 am. No sign of Hawk anywhere. "He'll be here," she said, opening the driver's side door.

Walking to the front door of her store, Nikki began to unlock it but found it open. "Hello, Lidia?" she called out, opening the door.

"Behind the counter," Lidia yelled back.

"You're early," Nikki said, closing the door and by cautious nature, locking it. Sure, in a small town like Maple Hills, there was no need to lock doors. But habit was a habit.

"Doing inventory," Lidia told Nikki as she watched her approach the counter, walking past wooden shelves holding a wide variety of chocolate candy bars ordered from different parts of the world: Holland, Germany, France, Russia, Israel, Switzerland. "I have to make sure the shelf life on our chocolates is okay."

"I see," Nikki said, impressed. Walking behind the front counter, she quickly placed her purse in the back office and returned to Lidia, complimenting her clothes.

"I like your outfit."

"Honey, I'm wearing a green t-shirt and a granny skirt," Lidia laughed. "If you admire this, then you need real help."

Nikki laughed. "I guess. Listen Lidia, Hawk Daily is supposed to be coming for coffee around nine."

Lidia stopped taking inventory. "Hawk Daily?" she asked in an uh-oh voice.

"What's the matter?"

Lidia scratched the back of her head with the pen she was holding. "Nikki, dear, people around town believe you're—"

"After a story. Yeah, I was told," Nikki told Lidia, rolling her eyes. "Lidia, there is much more going on here than people know. I thought about this last night while I was making chocolate, and I decided to take you into my confidence. You're an honest woman and about my only friend in town. I did have dinner with Jane, the lady who works at the hospital, and her husband last night. But that friendship will take time."

"I know the woman. She's very nice," Lidia told Nikki. "Her son has autism and lives in a facility in Boston."

"She told me," Nikki nodded her head. "I can't imagine how tough that must be for her and her husband."

"It must be tough. Now, getting back to Hawk Daily," Lidia said, putting the pad of paper down on the counter, "listen, you don't need to be seen with him. Why, people will think you really are after a story! Don't get me wrong, Hawk Daily is a nice man...a little handsome, but everyone knows Stacy Norton is after him. If a new woman, namely you, is seen on Hawk's arm, a woman everyone believes is after a story, it'll make Stacy Norton into your enemy and confirm what everyone in town is whispering about."

"Who is Stacy Norton?" Nikki asked, fighting back a smile. Small-town drama. Go figure.

"Stacy Norton is the richest woman in our fine little town," Lidia pointed out, "a black widow. She is forty-four years old, and she's already been through five husbands, taking all of them for every cent they owned."

"Lidia, I have other matters to worry about. Now listen to me, I need your help and—"

"Oh no, yesterday we agreed that my assistance remains

within the walls of this store," Lidia quickly objected. Grabbing the pad of paper, she quickly went back to work. "Now, where was I? Oh yes..."

Before Nikki could talk to Lidia, Hawk knocked on the front door of the store. "He's here. Will you let him in? I'll go make the coffee."

Lidia cast Nikki a strong, disapproving eye. "I warned you."

"And I'm thankful," Nikki said, motioning toward the front door with her hands. "Now please, unlock the front door."

11

"Yeah, yeah," Lidia said, shaking her head. She walked off, mumbling to herself.

"Hey, hey," Hawk said, walking up to the front counter after Lidia let him in, "right on time. So where's that coffee?"

"Making it now," Nikki said, walking out from behind the counter.

"My, you look pretty...friendly," Hawk told Nikki, throwing his hands up into the air.

"Thank you," Nikki offered a polite smile. "Uh, can we take a walk while we're waiting for the coffee?"

"Sure," Hawk said, bowing his arm toward the front door, "after you."

Nikki told Lidia she would be back in about half an hour and walked Hawk outside onto the front sidewalk. "Anything on Denforth yet?" she asked, deliberately baiting Hawk.

"Nah," Hawk said, throwing his hands down into the pockets of his jeans, "we're off the case. Feds took it over."

The blue and red football jersey Hawk was wearing made him look like a jock instead of a detective. "Forgive me for saying this, but you're not the normal detective type. What I mean is, the NYPD type."

"I wasn't," Hawk laughed. "You see, Pop and Mom divorced when I was a kid. Mom was in the Navy. I tagged around with her all over the place. Before Mom passed away from breast cancer, she made me promise that I would get closer to Pop. So, here I am, fulfilling that promise."

"Your mother lived in New York, then, right?"

"Smart lady, give her a cracker," Hawk nodded his head, walking with Nikki past the sleepy stores. "Mom liked the city. I hated it. But when I met my ex-wife, the odds were really against me. No man can stand up against two stubborn women."

Nikki smiled. "I guess not."

"Mom was a good woman. She had a good sense of humor."

"I'm sorry you lost her," Nikki told Hawk.

"So am I," Hawk said, kicking at a cigarette butt some tourist had tossed down onto the sidewalk.

"Listen," Nikki said, grabbing Hawk's arm, "I...can I confide in you? I mean, can we create a friendship of confidence and trust?"

"I'm not a psychiatrist, but I can give it my best shot," Hawk said, turning his head to the side and studying Nikki's face. "What you mean is you want to tell me something that you don't want me throwing at Pop."

"At anyone," Nikki told Hawk. "Please, Hawk."

Hawk took a deep breath, removed his hands from the pocket of his jeans, scratched the back of his head, smiled, and said sure. "You can trust me if you want."

"I believe I can," Nikki replied, staring into Hawk's eyes. The man had an honest way to him that appealed to her. "Hawk, Steven Denforth is not who you think he is. Keep walking with me and I'll explain."

Hawk listened to Nikki explain about Hanz Hochberg, about his parents, about the paper, the fire, Wendy Phillips, ending with finding Adal and Johan missing from her guestroom. "Who's the real detective?" Hawk said, absorbing every word Nikki revealed to him.

"They believe the killer is in town. I believe that, too," Nikki said, stopping in front of a small bakery. Local store owners were beginning to arrive. All businesses on the main strip opened at 10:00 am. Thinking about what Lidia told her, Nikki edged Hawk back to her store before too many people saw them together. "If you can check out all the people Hanz wrote about, see if those people are in town, where they were at the time of the hit-and-run, and if any of them have left town, that would be great."

"And you?" Hawk asked, walking back into Nikki's store.

"I'm going to pay Wendy Phillips a visit. The paper is up and running. I'm sure she works there," Nikki explained.

"Yes, Wendy Phillips is currently employed at the paper," Hawk confirmed, walking up to the front counter. Spotting Lidia, he smiled. "Mrs. Green, good morning."

Lidia frowned. "Kinda early to be chasing the new woman in town, isn't it?"

"We're merely friends," Hawk said, throwing his hands into the air again.

"Lidia, pour Detective Daily a cup of coffee, okay?" Nikki pleaded.

"Black, no cream or sugar," Hawk told Lidia and tossed her a wink.

"What about you, dear?" Lidia asked Nikki, making a snarly face at Hawk.

"A little cream and sugar will be fine," Nikki told Lidia, desperately trying to prevent an overprotective mother figure from embarrassing her. After Lidia walked away to the back office, Nikki let out her breath. Letting her eyes wander around the store, she studied the chocolates. "Sometimes I wonder how I went from being a journalist in Atlanta to baking chocolate in a small town in Vermont."

Hawk pointed up at the ceiling. "God has a way of things," he smiled. "So now, tell me, why should I let you go speak to Wendy Phillips alone?"

"Hanz Hochberg remained in town after he burned down the building his paper was located in. Why? I keep thinking about what Johan Hochberg said last night. Maybe Wendy Phillips was blackmailing him to stay in town? Maybe she was trying to force Hanz to take her with him? There are many possibilities. I have to find out."

"Do you think she killed Hanz Hochberg?" Hawk openly asked.

"No," Nikki confessed. "Listen, Hawk, let me try to get

some answers from her, okay? You investigate the people Hanz wrote about."

"You make a good boss," Hawk told Nikki, caving into her request. "Okay, sister, this is how we're gonna work this deal. You handle Phillips, and I'll handle the people this Hanz joker blackmailed. But you listen and listen carefully, Phillips is as far as you go, are we clear? Someone killed Hanz Hochberg, which means they can and will kill again if pushed into a corner."

"I know," Nikki answered nervously. "That fact is cemented deep into my soul."

Lidia appeared from the back office holding two brown mugs. "Here," she said, handing Hawk his coffee.

"Thanks."

'Thank you, Lidia," Nikki said, taking her coffee.

"Don't thank me yet. I heard what you two were talking about. I guess I better go with you to see Wendy Phillips. I don't want you alone," Lidia told Nikki and then let her shoulders slump. "All I wanted was a quiet, part-time job."

"Thanks," Nikki told Lidia. Reaching out, she hugged the woman. "We'll go see Wendy Phillips after we close today. It'll be wise for me to spend the day in my store, just in case someone is watching."

"I agree," Hawk told Nikki, sipping his coffee. "Well, I got a lot of footwork today, so I better beat it. I'll call you later. Maybe we can get a bite to eat...as friends."

Nikki smiled. "My house, nine sharp. We'll have a late dinner...as friends," she told Hawk. "But first, do me this favor." Nikki walked to Hawk and whispered in his ear.

"Will do," Hawk promised. Finishing his coffee, he

handed the mug back to Lidia. "Not bad. See you for dinner," he told Nikki and then tipped Lidia a wink.

"Not bad," Lidia fussed, watching Hawk walk out of the store, clearly making her voice reach the man's ears. But as soon as he was out of sight, she smiled. "He's a little charming...not much, but some."

"We're just friends," Nikki promised. "You know my divorce was messy. I'm not ready to open my heart again, not right now. And with that said, let's get to work and hope today will be a good one."

"Well, it'll just be you and me. While you were out walking with Mr. Not Bad, our young friend called in," Lidia explained. "Her aunt is sick again. Tori has to stay home and tend to her. If you ask me, that woman is about as sick as a tiger sneezing at an innocent mouse."

Nikki patted Lidia's shoulder. "We have to work on Tori. Oh, if I could adopt her and make her my own! I'll give her a call later."

Following Nikki behind the front counter, Lidia went back to her inventory. Even though her face didn't show it, she was very scared. Everything inside her yelled that the person who ran down Steven Denforth—or Hanz Hochberg, or whatever the man's name was—was a local.

After opening the store, Nikki and Lidia waited for a few minutes, and then, right on time, tourists began to trickle in, slowly at first and then in a steady stream. But even dealing with a store full of tourists couldn't take Nikki's mind off the killing. As far as she knew, any person who entered her store could be the killer.

12

"Whew," Nikki said, wiping sweat from her face as she locked the front door, "what a day."

"Tell me about it," Lidia said, plopping down in a wooden chair behind the front counter. "Are you sure we have to go see Wendy Phillips? I'm bushed. Herbert will want his dinner, too."

"Yes, I'm sure," Nikki told Lidia, walking back to the counter. "I'll count the drawer down and close out the credit card machine. After I get the deposit ready, we'll run over to the bank and then hit the paper. It's only four. The paper is open until six."

"Okay," Lidia caved in. Rubbing her ankles, she watched Nikki walk around the counter and take the cash drawer from the antique cash register. "I'll sweep up some."

"You rest," Nikki ordered Lidia. "I'll hurry."

After counting the cash drawer down and closing out the credit card machine, Nikki quickly prepared the daily deposit and hurried out of the store with Lidia. "We'll take my SUV," she told Lidia.

"Uh-oh," Lidia said, motioning to a woman walking down the sidewalk, "here comes Stacy Norton."

Nikki looked up the sidewalk. A beautiful blond woman wearing a loose, flowy white dress was approaching her. The woman screamed of money and many, many plastic surgeries. "Nikki Bates?"

"Yes," Nikki said, unlocking the driver's side door to the SUV.

"My name is Stacy Norton. It has been brought to my attention that you have been seen with Hawk Daily."

Lidia stepped back. Nikki was on her own. Curious to see how her boss was going to handle Stacy Norton, she braced for a cat fight. "I have," Nikki told Stacy. Turning to face the woman, she stepped forward. "Hawk and I are engaged to be married, but that's our little secret. We're running away tonight to tie the knot. I wanted a church wedding, but you know Hawk, always in a rush to do things."

"Well!" Stacy huffed, feeling her cheeks flame red.

"I know," Nikki said, really pouring it on, "Hawk didn't give me much notice, either. All he said is we had to hurry and get married because there's a black widow in town after him and...oh, oh dear—you and Hawk—was he meaning you? I'm so sorry. Me and my big mouth."

"You vicious little snake," Stacy snarled at Nikki. Spinning around, she stormed off.

Slapping her leg, Lidia burst out laughing. "That was wonderful, honey. My, you really shut her up!"

"Hop in," Nikki grinned, watching Stacy storm away. Certain she would see Stacy Norton again, she climbed into the driver's seat and drove away toward the bank, weaving through thick lines of traffic created by tired tourists leaving town to find somewhere to eat dinner.

After dropping the deposit off at the bank, Nikki drove to the local newspaper. Pulling up in front of a newly built red brick building, she parked next to a red BMW. "You don't have to come in."

"I'm not," Lidia told Nikki, folding her arms together. "I'm going to sit right here. If you're not out in thirty minutes, then I'm coming in."

"You're the best," Nikki told Lidia. Staring at the brick building she braced herself. "Wendy Phillips may become hostile. What can you tell me about her?"

"I don't know much," Lidia confessed. "She's married to Brent Phillips...I don't know anything about him. She has no children. She's about thirty-five, I guess. Went to college in Boston...not sure why she came back here to Maple Hills? Maybe her husband? From the few times I met her, she seemed nice. Herbert likes to sell his junk, so I've been in the paper a few times to have his junk put in the 'For Sale' section. The old building was a lot nicer; it had more character and—"

"Thanks," Nikki said, noticing Lidia veering off track and cutting her off.

"Oh, sure, honey," Lidia blushed. "The older I get, the more my mind seems to wander."

"I'll be a few minutes." Opening the driver's side door, Nikki studied the brick building with calm eyes. Nodding her head, she walked up to a glass door and without hesitating, walked into a front lobby that smelled of peppermint and ink. Wendy Phillips was sitting behind a polished wooden counter lined with fake plants and a bowl holding cinnamon and peppermint candy. When she saw Nikki, her face became red.

13

Nikki walked over a polished wooden floor, glancing around the stylish lobby that reminded her of the lobby at the hospital. Approaching the counter, she focused her attention on Wendy Phillips. To her surprise, the woman was not very pretty. She saw a woman with short brown hair and a skinny face scarred from years of acne. Even though the woman tried to dress in a stylish red pantsuit, she looked cheap and fake. Nikki wondered what a man like Hanz Hochberg saw in a woman like this. "Wendy Phillips?"

"Get out of here before I call the cops," Wendy snapped at Nikki, standing up from her office chair.

With the counter separating them, Nikki felt comfortable to continue speaking. Besides, even if Wendy Phillips attacked her, she could hold her own against the skinny woman. Wanting to avoid a physical fight, though, Nikki cautioned herself to walk on egg shells. "I only need to ask you a few questions."

"Get out," Wendy said, throwing her right index finger at the front door.

"Does the name Hanz Hochberg mean anything to you?"

Preparing to yell at Nikki again, Wendy froze. Her scarred face went blank. "You know? I thought you came in here to question me...people are saying you are after a story." Glancing over her shoulder to make sure the door leading into the paper was closed, Wendy threw her thumbnail into her mouth and began chewing away. "I didn't kill him."

"I don't think you did," Nikki assured Wendy, "but someone did, and I'd like to help the police find that person. Wendy, you helped Hanz write those awful stories, didn't you?"

Wendy began to object but then simply nodded her head yes. "You can't tell anyone, okay? My husband will kill me."

"How did you and Hanz Hochberg meet?"

"In Atlantic City," Wendy said, still chewing on her thumbnail. "My husband was playing at the craps table. He was on a hot streak. I was standing off to the side, sipping some champagne."

"Go on," Nikki carefully urged Wendy.

"This man walks up to me and begins talking to me," Wendy explained, lowering her voice to a whisper. Nikki moved closer to her. "He was very handsome. He actually began flirting with me. I was flattered."

"What about your husband?"

"He would have killed me," Wendy admitted, "but Mr. Luck was too busy at the table to know if I was alive or not. I want to divorce him, but I...I can't. While he gambled, I spent time with Hanz. I talked a lot. I...kinda slipped up and told Hanz that I had money, though. But at the time, it didn't seem to matter. A handsome man was showing me attention. I really wanted to impress him. And when Hanz suggested he visit me here in Maple Hills, I was thrilled."

"I heard you went to college in Boston. How did you end up back here in Maple Hills?" Nikki asked the quick side question.

"I met my husband here when I came home to visit my parents. He was my dad's accountant. My parents were very rich—"

"Were?" Nikki interrupted.

"My parents died a year apart from each other, my mother of cancer and my father of a brain aneurysm," Wendy explained. "They left me everything, and stupid me really believed my husband loved me instead of the money. And then I blabbed my mouth to Hanz about my money, too."

"Why can't you divorce your husband?"

"No prenuptial agreement," Wendy admitted miserably. "I'm not about to let that slime-ball get half of what's mine."

"Go on," Nikki told Wendy. "What about Hanz?"

"Oh, Mr. Sweet-talker," Wendy said in a disgusted tone. "I thought he really loved me, but I was wrong...really wrong."

"It happens. Keep going."

"Well, at first Hanz and I spent some quiet time alone. I rented him a cabin outside of town. That should have been my first red flag, but I was too blind to see. I would take trips out to see him. We talked...well, I talked," Wendy told

Nikki, leaning her head close. "Anyway, one night I began talking about how much I wanted to divorce my husband. I really blabbed my mouth a lot, complained about the people in this town. Hanz was patient. He would ask me a few questions, listen to me fuss, and then ask me a few more questions."

"Baiting you. Go on," Nikki told Wendy.

"I see that now," Wendy agreed, "but I thought he loved me. When he went a week without talking to me, I became worried. But then he called me here at the paper."

"Why?"

"Hanz said he wanted me to do him a favor, but the idea involved me buying the paper for him. Somehow he had the money. He invited me out to his cabin and explained his plans. At first, I was totally against it, but Hanz kept sweet-talking me. He told me we would use the blackmail money to run away together, and like a dummy, I believed him. I didn't want to help him, but I was so desperate for Hanz to love me, to be proud of me...I just couldn't say no, even though the names Hanz gave me were people my husband knew. But Hanz controlled the staff, and I was ordered to tell them to do what he said or take a hike. No one wanted to get fired, so they kept their mouths shut and did as they were told. At night, Hanz would come in through the back door, and we would work on the stories together."

"How did your husband know the people Hanz targeted?"

"My husband is an accountant and works for the people Hanz and I wrote about," Wendy explained. Nervously, she looked over her shoulder. "I told Hanz, maybe we needed to write about other people, but he insisted. He had a list of people and was determined not to write about anyone else...I don't know how he came up with the people he did. It worried me because they were connected to my husband, but I was so taken with Hanz—his charm and fake promises that everything was going to be okay—I went through with it."

"Everyone on Hanz's list was featured in the paper?"

"Almost," Wendy explained and then frowned. "One day, Hanz tells me our fun time is over. With no explanation, he burns down the old building. Then he..."

"Then he what?"

"Threatens to blackmail me. He played me the entire time. He had evidence against me that could have landed me in jail," Wendy whispered. "The amount of money he was demanding...I told him it would take time. I couldn't just waltz up to the bank and take out wads of cash. My husband would have suspected something. So I kept paying for the rental cabin outside of town he was staying in and asked him to be patient with me. Hanz didn't like being delayed. He got very angry with me."

"How did he threaten you?"

"He threatened to kill me," Wendy frowned again. "My miserable husband would take every cent I own if I ended up six feet under. I had no choice but to do what Hanz wanted. I should have known something was wrong when he refused to tell me where he was going with the blackmail money. I was just glad that my husband was staying out of town a lot."

"I don't understand."

"Atlantic City, gambling," Wendy pointed out the obvious. "I told you I have money, but yet, here I am working. Why? Because my husband gambles our money away. For once I was grateful he was in Atlantic City…I really thought Hanz loved me and was going to take me away. He turned out to be a creep."

"He used you. My guess is you gave him a clear shot at blackmailing you, and you didn't even know it."

Wendy lowered her head in shame. "I sold the paper to Benjamin Westmore, acting as a go-between for Hanz, telling Mr. Westmore that Hanz—er, Steven—had left town out of fear for his life. I managed to talk Mr. Westmore into giving me a job, the same crummy job. Now Hanz is dead, I'm still stuck with my lousy husband, and the people of this town still treat me like dirt. I'm back at square one. At least I'm not being blackmailed anymore. I guess when my husband gets back from Atlantic City I'll go back to being his doormat."

"Your husband has been in Atlantic City this entire time?"

"No, he came back the night Hanz burned down the paper," Wendy explained.

14

Looking at a white clock hanging on the wall over the reception area, Nikki knew she had to pick up the pace. "Hurting people is never the right answer," Nikki told Wendy. "What you did, using the press to hurt people, embarrass them, blackmail them, was morally and ethically wrong. I know you had your reasons, but no reason is good enough to hurt people."

"Are you going to turn me in?" Wendy asked fearfully.

"First, let's talk about Mr. and Mrs. Hochberg," Nikki said, hurriedly pushing the conversation along.

Wendy quit chewing her thumbnail and tossed her chin into her shaky hands. Looking down at the counter, she shook her head. "They pushed me into a corner. I never knew people could gather all that evidence against me. They knew my every coming and going...scary! But, all that old couple wanted was for me to set up a meeting between them and their son."

"Why my store?"

"Hanz had a sweet tooth," Wendy explained in a simple tone. "Mr. and Mrs. Hochberg were very stern with me. They understood what kind of woman I was. Oh, the look that old woman gave me...I'll never be able to live it down."

"Wendy, who killed Hanz Hochberg?" Nikki asked in a stern voice.

"I don't know," Wendy said, raising her eyes up to Nikki. Nikki saw that the woman was about ready to burst into tears. "Hanz never admitted that he was threatened, but he torched the old building. Every bit of printing equipment—files, computers, everything."

"I see," Nikki said as a new thought struck her mind. "Okay, here's what I'm going to do. I'm going to forget I ever spoke to you about this matter, okay? I think you learned your lesson. Sending you to jail will only destroy your life. But we're going to talk more, not about Hanz but about you. I want to help you, Wendy. I want to be your friend if you allow me."

"You want to be my friend? Why?" Wendy asked, feeling the tears begin to leave her scared eyes.

"I can tell all you want is to be loved. You're full of pain and anger, but you're not a bad person. Yes, what you did was wrong, but we can move past that, okay? Please, allow me to be your friend."

"And if I say no you go blab everything we talked about to Chief Daily, right?"

"If you say no, I walk out of here and say nothing. If you want to accept my offer, please come to my store tomorrow near lunch. We'll sneak off and grab a burger together," Nikki

Raspberry Truffle Murder

said. Reaching across the counter, she wiped Wendy's tears away. "We have to find the real you. The you I see right now looks very cheap and very fake. If I see that, other people see it. Let's find the real you...the beautiful you, okay?"

"Okay," Wendy said, fighting back her tears. "But what about—"

"One step at a time," Nikki smiled, wiping more tears away. "Now I have to go. But I'll see you tomorrow for lunch, right?"

"Yeah...yes, sure," Wendy smiled through her tears.

"Great," Nikki smiled, "I'll see you then. And by the way, it's my treat. Oh, one last question?"

"Sure, I guess."

"Who were you going to write about next, before Hanz burned down the building?"

Wendy glanced around, made sure no one was listening and told Nikki who the next victim was going to be. "A bit too late, but it would have been nice."

"Why the mayor?"

Making a sour face, Wendy quickly explained why she had chosen the mayor to be her next target. "Hanz didn't agree. The following night he burned down the building."

"Thank you," Nikki told Wendy, feeling her gut catch the killer.

Waving goodbye, she hurried outside and jumped into the driver's seat of the SUV and buckled up. "I think I know who killed Hanz Hochberg," she told Lidia in an excited voice.

"Who?" Lidia begged.

"Not yet, I need to talk to Hawk. I'll drop you off at your car, okay?"

"Not on your life. I want to know who the killer is," Lidia told Nikki and buckled her seat belt. "Herbert can wait for his dinner tonight."

15

Backing out into the street, Nikki aimed the SUV back toward her store. "Lidia, I need some background information, but this time, we'll skip the library. Instead, let's go to my place. I downloaded the photos I took of the newspapers onto my computer. I need to check something."

"Why on earth did you leave your job in Atlanta? You seem like a fish out of water in Maple Hills," Lidia asked Nikki.

"I needed a change," Nikki confessed, biting down hard on her lip. "After the divorce, it just made sense to take a different path. I miss working for the paper, but then again, I don't. The paper became so political I was having my back pushed into a corner every step I took. So I left the paper and moved here."

Lidia studied Nikki's face. She saw flashes of anger, pain, regret, sadness and remorse flash across the woman's eyes. "Are you okay, dear?"

Nikki shrugged her shoulders as she drove out of town, grateful that most of the tourist traffic had thinned out. "It's everywhere. You can't really hide from it."

"What?"

"The reality of life," Nikki explained. "Every second is like a new snapshot you take with your eyes, and your memory collects those snapshots and creates a photo album. Sadly, most of the photos hidden in the albums of our memories are photos we wish to forget. I guess that sounds pretty pessimistic and gloomy, huh?"

"Tell that to the evening news," Lidia told Nikki and patted her arm.

Nikki didn't speak again until she pulled up in her driveway and saw Hawk leaning against a red Jeep, waiting for her. "You're kinda early for dinner," she said, walking up to Hawk.

"I got a rough call," Hawk told Nikki in a voice that wasn't happy. With his arms folded over his chest, he watched Lidia get out of the SUV.

"Let's go inside," Nikki suggested. "I have something—"

Hawk shook his head no. "Everyone Hanz Hochberg wrote about is still living in town. Every last person nearly slammed a door in my face. Can't say I blame them. I got a few tidbits from them, but not much. But let me tell you, every last one of them reassured me they were leaving town as soon as the air clears. Hanz Hochberg really hit the nail on the head with those slugs."

"Actually, Wendy Phillips hit the nail on the head, but keep going," Nikki urged Hawk, reading the deep anger in his eyes. The man was obviously ready to kick a tree down.

"Dr. Mayton—that slime-ball, thief, wife beater, drug addict, liar, lousy doctor. Mandy Long, suspected of embezzlement; her husband died under suspicious conditions, and she collected insurance money from the man's death. Jack Taylor: a corrupt judge kicked off the bench for taking bribes, spent a few days in jail for threatening to kill his wife," Hawk told Nikki, unfolding his arms and slapping his fingers one by one as he named off names.

"I read the articles written on them," Nikki told Hawk as a cool breeze touched her face. "Hawk, what's bothering you? Low-life criminals don't bother a man like you."

"Spit it out," Lidia fussed at Hawk.

Hawk shook his head and began to pace around. "My last visit was to Dr. Mayton, again," Hawk explained. "I started noticing a pattern with the people I talked to."

Nikki felt her hands begin to tingle. She, too, had noticed a pattern. "Every person written about serves on the city council. Every person written about supported the mayor's re-election. Every person written about came from Boston. The mayor is from Boston."

"And lo and behold, who calls me and yells at me to back off questioning his precious little birdies?" Hawk asked Nikki, squeezing his hands into two tight fists. "I don't like a weasel pushing my shoulders when I'm conducting an investigation. I push back. Anyway, I was talking to Dr. Mayton about why and how he ended up on the city council. A man trying to hide his past, hiding out in a small town, would try and stay as low-key as possible."

"What was his answer?" Nikki asked.

"I didn't get an answer. The mayor called my cell phone before that rat could answer me," Hawk stormed. "Doesn't matter. I gave strict orders for all of them to remain in town. My gut told me who killed Hanz Hochberg."

"Who? For crying out loud, who?" Lidia begged.

"The mayor," Nikki told Lidia. "Wendy Phillips—or maybe Hanz Hochberg—deliberately left clues connecting the people they wrote about to the mayor. I didn't see the connection at first, but after speaking with Wendy Phillips, she confirmed my suspicion. Actually, Mrs. Slokam set the ball rolling. For a sweet old librarian, she sure was intent on protecting those papers. Seemed strange to me that she could call Chief Daily in the middle of a murder and have him rush to the library, too. Unless she was protecting her husband, Mayor Slokam. It began with Dr. Mayton calling me. Why? How did he find out I was snooping around? And how did he get my cell phone number?"

"I always knew that woman was a two-faced liar," Lidia burst out. "I never liked her, no sir, never."

"Wendy Phillips told me that Hanz Hochberg suddenly stopped the articles and burned down the building housing the paper," Nikki explained, glancing up into a relaxed blue sky. *God is an amazing artist*, she mused, taking the time to collect her thoughts. Here she was, surrounded by a rough and delicate beauty so intermingled that it was impossible to tell where the brush of the artist began and the canvas ended. "Hawk, did you do me that favor I asked?"

"Yeah," Hawk told Nikki, pulling a small notepad from his front pocket. "I checked into Wendy Phillips' husband. A real lowlife by the name of Brent Phillips. Got busted running books for the Bonaduci family in Boston, did a little time in his early twenties. After he got out of prison, he spent a few years in Germany on a work program and—"

"That's it!" Nikki yelled.

"What's it?" Lidia yelled back.

"That's the key," Nikki said and hugged Hawk. "That's how Hanz met Wendy in Atlantic City. He was there to meet her husband. Hanz had to flee New York before the German authorities could catch him, and I bet he called Wendy's husband. How else could they be in Atlantic City at the same time?"

"Keep going, you bloodhound," Hawk grinned.

Nikki began pacing. "Hawk, remember what Dr. Mayton confessed to me, about stealing money from the mob? I think he said it was in 1982."

"Yeah," Hawk nodded his head, "I squeezed that out of him, too. The rat claims he didn't steal from the Bonaduci family, though—some other New York mob family. That guy has many faces and a lot of lies. Who knows?"

"Every person Hanz targeted in the paper..." Nikki said, thinking. And then every piece of the puzzle fell into her lap. "Hawk, in 1984 the Bonaduci family left New York and relocated to Boston. My father always kept up with the mob families. He took down the DeDonato family in Atlanta—a small crime family trying to dig in, never made headlines."

"Everyone the German wrote about is from Boston," Hawk said, rubbing his chin. "Nikki, are you trying to say we have members of the Bonaduci family living right here in Maple Hills?"

"Run their prints and find out. It's possible Dr. Mayton

did steal money from another mob family. The Bonaduci family was falling apart at that time and had to rebuild in Boston," Nikki told Hawk. "My gut is telling me Hanz and Brent Phillips came up with a real get-rich-quick scheme. Hanz would write the stories, shake the people he targeted up a little, demand money, and then kill Wendy. He would then blame her murder on the people he wrote about, exposing them as a mob family. Wendy's husband collects her money, splits it with Hanz, and they're gone with the wind. That's why Brent Phillips had been out of town in Atlantic City and just so happened to come back the night Hanz burned down the paper. Hanz called him back into town."

"Why?" Hawk asked, running just a tad behind Nikki's thinking.

"Why didn't Mayor Slokam shut down the paper when the first story appeared? Lidia, you told me he seemed very interested in protecting the stories. He was probably in on the entire deal, being paid off to keep the paper open instead of having it shut down," Nikki replied.

"So why kill Hanz Hochberg?" Hawk asked.

"Well, I'm sure the mayor wasn't the man behind the wheel of the black SUV that ran Hans Hochberg down. The man behind the wheel was Brent Phillips. The black SUV was a rental, probably from Atlantic City."

"I'll check into that," Hawk promised.

"The mayor had Hanz Hochberg killed because suddenly, trying to frame the Bonaduci family for murder didn't seem like such a good idea," Nikki continued, going off on a gut feeling. "My bet is he got a nasty call from an angry old man wearing a very nice Italian suit in Boston who told him to try thinking differently, which would explain why Mrs. Slokam acted the way she did. I guess she was only worried about her husband's welfare, really. Check the mayor's cell phone, okay, Hawk?"

"I will. Now answer me this: Why did Brent Phillips return to town the night Hanz Hochberg torched the newspaper?" Hawk asked.

"Hanz must have called him. The mayor probably called Brent Phillips and demanded a meeting and called the whole thing off, throwing out some threats," Nikki explained. "Most of this is speculation, but we'll soon back it up with proof. Let's go see the mayor after you run his cell phone. I'm sure you know some people in New York who can do you that favor and save us the time of having a judge issue a court order for Mayor Slokam's cell phone records."

"I do," Hawk grinned. "I'll also have some of my old buddies send me every photo of the Bonaduci family. Maybe that will save us the time of running the fingerprints."

"My goodness," Lidia said, rubbing her head, "what a tangled mess. I could never be a detective."

Nikki threw her arm around Lidia and walked her inside the cabin. "Let's go have some coffee and chocolate and wait to see what Hawk comes up with on his end. We can't push the mayor into a tight corner without proof. A smart detective waits to pounce only when he—or she—has a trap set."

"I guess Herbert's dinner is really going to be late," Lidia told Nikki. "Oh well, I guess we can grill some burgers under the moon later tonight."

As Nikki and Lidia walked inside, Hawk snatched out his cell phone and made a call. "Okay pretty woman," he whispered at Nikki, "let me see what I can do, and maybe win your heart in the process."

16

Wendy Phillips hated pulling down the long concrete driveway leading to the dark, two-story home. It wasn't that she didn't like her house—the house simply was cold, devoid of love and warmth, and sad. She only wanted a man to love her and help her fill a home with the sound of many children laughing and playing. Wendy felt like crying as she parked her car in front of a wooden carport. "I guess you're still in Atlantic City," she said, looking at the dark front windows of the house. "Someday I'll find love...wait and see."

Wendy turned off the car, got out and started to walk down a pebbled pathway leading to the front door. Movement caught her eye. Pausing, she glanced to the far corner of the carport. "Hello?" she called out. Only the whisper of wind playing in the sleepy trees answered. Suddenly living eight miles from town at the end of a long road surrounded by woods didn't seem like such a good idea. Sure, her husband had insisted on the house because of the privacy it offered, but the jerk never left enough money to install outside lights and complained if she left on a single light when she left the house. And now, there she was, standing in the dark with only a half moon sitting in a partly clouded sky as her only light. "Hello?"

Slowly, a tall, thin, old man walked into the open. "Hello, Mrs. Phillips," Mayor Slokam said in a voice that sounded like an undertaker.

"Mayor Slokam?" Wendy asked, feeling her blood turn cold.

"Yes, it's me," Mayor Slokam said, slowly approaching Wendy.

Resembling a mortician, Mayor Slokam walked forward like a man preparing to steal a corpse. With thin gray hair and a skeletal face, he always appeared creepy to Wendy. Never caring for the man, she kept her distance from him. But now here he was, walking toward her through the dark. "How...can I help you?"

"I'm in quite a mess," Mayor Slokam informed Wendy in a calm tone. "What began as a simple plan has transformed into a complicated matter."

"I'm afraid I don't understand," Wendy said, beginning to back away toward the front door of her home.

"Oh, you do," Mayor Slokam said. "You assisted our friend, Hanz Hochberg, in blackmailing certain members of the community. Members, I might mention, who have been pressing me into the floor for years. Foolishly, due to Mr. Hochberg and your husband, I thought I saw a way to be free of those vermin. They're like roaches really—one comes into town, and then another. I ended up with five roaches in my town and two very sneaky skunks who believed I was a fool. Oh, I let you write the stories, Mrs. Phillips. I also knew I was your last victim. Oh yes, I knew what Mr. Hochberg and your husband were up to. They were going to betray me in the end, blame the articles on me..."

"I don't understand," Wendy said, becoming even more frightened.

"Mr. Hochberg was going to kill you, and your husband was going to split your money with him. Your death was going to be blamed on me. Oh yes, your husband told me," Mayor Slokam explained, stopping a few feet from Wendy. "You were going to expose the Bonaduci family in the article you were going to write about me, casting full blame on myself, clearly making me the target. Out of revenge, I kill you and then kill myself. Quite a clever plan Mr. Hanz and your husband came up with."

"Please..." Wendy begged, watching Mayor Slokam pull a gun from the pocket of his blue suit.

"I saw Nikki Bates enter the paper's office earlier today."

"I didn't talk to her, I swear. I only told her what she wanted to hear. She knew about Hanz," Wendy said as tears began to fall from her eyes. "Please, don't kill me. I'm sorry..."

"Your husband had a change of heart, though. I started to become suspicious, so I made a little call to Boston and spoke with Mr. Bonaduci. He, in turn, sent someone to Atlantic City to have a chat with your husband. Your husband was, let's say, persuaded to confess the truth. I must admit, it was foolish to play with the children of a black widow, but I convinced Mr. Bonaduci that I was the victim. I was given a choice, one simple choice: Kill Hanz Hochberg."

"So why do you want to kill me?" Wendy cried.

"Your articles did have quite an effect," Mayor Slokam smiled. "Mr. Bonaduci was none too pleased about having his hidden children written about, his bad little children he has to hide. Now, poor Mr. Bonaduci has to relocate his children to another town. You can clearly see my disappointment of losing such quality citizens who have spent years forcing me to do their bidding, including forcing the hospital to hire a doctor whose license was revoked for malpractice. Do you realize the criminal punishment I could face?"

"So they're splitting town," Wendy said, flinching as Mayor Slokam aimed the gun at her. "That's good news, right? Hanz is dead, and that's good news, too…right?"

"Your husband is now also among the deceased," Mayor Slokam added. "He did my bidding. He ran down Hanz Hochberg and returned to Atlantic City like a good boy, only to face his own demise. You're the only loose end I have. You see, I had your husband convince Hans Hochberg to burn down the paper and forget the entire…shall we say, deal."

"Hanz wasn't stupid," Wendy said, waiting to be shot. With her heart racing, she held her hands up in front of her face.

"Oh, your husband convinced Hanz that the FBI got wise to the situation and was moving into town. Hanz was warned to leave, but he didn't, did he?"

"He blackmailed me for money. He was hanging around

until I could get the money for him," Wendy explained, hoping her words would buy her a few more precious seconds of life.

"Ah, so he didn't want to leave empty-handed, was that it?" Mayor Slokam said, amused. "Well, he should have left town when he had the chance. I arranged for your husband to take him back to Atlantic City and...dispose of him. But then, Hanz simply vanished into thin air, now didn't he?"

"I...he was staying at a cabin I rented for him."

"I see," Mayor Slokam said, "I assumed you had something to do with it. I had your husband watch your house. We saw the German couple visit you. Very curious. That's when I devised a plan. You see, I had your house wired. I heard you arrange for Hanz to meet his parents in town. With it being tourist season, well, a hit-and-run seemed just right. Your husband runs down Hanz Hochberg and makes a quick escape back to Atlantic City."

"Please..." Wendy said, begging for her life again. "I was wrong to help Hanz...I was wrong to..." With nothing left to say, she dropped to her knees. Throwing her hands over her face, she cried, "Oh, go ahead and kill me then."

"In time. But first, I want the blackmail money. Oh yes, I know you have it."

Wendy shook her head no. "No, I don't. Hanz took it...I don't know where the money is."

"Young lady, I can either make your death very painful or very easy, the choice is yours. Now tell me where the blackmail money is," Mayor Slokam said, turning his voice dark and cruel.

"Check the cabin, maybe it's all there," Wendy cried. "I

promise you, I don't have the money. I drove to Boston to get the money, but I gave every cent to Hanz."

Mayor Slokam shook his head irritably. "This is my town, Mrs. Phillips. I am finally free of the vermin that has infested Maple Hills. I, too, had an agenda. That is why I supported the writing of the articles against the wishes of the town while creating the idea that any citizen could be targeted next. I played the town against itself, forced people to lose trust in each other while at the same time allowing the stories to continue to benefit myself. Of course, I was being hammered by Mayton and the others on my end, but I played dumb well enough. I told them I had to let the stories continue or else Hanz Hochberg—or Steven Denforth—might print the actual truth about their identities instead of just a few damaging tidbits connected to their past lives. They, of course, did not know I knew they were being blackmailed."

"Please, I won't say anything," Wendy begged, raising her head.

"Oh, how sweet it was watching those vermin sweat," Mayor Slokam smiled, keeping the gun in his hand aimed at Wendy. "But the time came to end the fun when Mr. Hanz made the horrible mistake and cast suspicion on himself."

"What did he do?" Wendy asked, realizing that begging for her life was futile.

"His body language changed," Mayor Slokam answered Wendy. "I may be old, but I am not foolish. Hanz Hochberg believed himself to be a genius, but with age comes the ability to read the human body. Hanz Hochberg was the fool in the end. Now, enough talk. Mrs. Phillips, I want to know where the blackmail money is. I will not ask again."

Before Wendy could speak, the sound of approaching sirens filled the air. Mayor Slokam spun around and peered down the long driveway. With his back turned, Wendy eased to her feet, darted forward with her hands out and shoved Mayor Slokam in the back as hard as she could. The old man went flying forward and then tumbled down onto the concrete driveway. Not wasting any time, Wendy ran for her house and managed to get through the front door.

Moaning in pain, Mayor Slokam grabbed his back. Unable to move, he knew it was over. Yes, he thought he had outwitted his enemies, but in the end, a simple bad back had ended him. A minute later, a red Jeep with a red bubble flashing on the dashboard zoomed up the driveway, followed by three police cars. Hawk jumped out of the Jeep with his gun drawn. "Don't move," he yelled at Mayor Slokam.

"My back," Mayor Slokam moaned in pain.

Easing forward, Hawk grabbed the gun Mayor Slokam had terrorized Wendy with. "Nikki, check the house."

Climbing out of the Jeep, Nikki ran to the front door of the house and called out Wendy's name. The front door flew open, and Wendy ran into Nikki's arms. "He tried to kill me!" she cried.

Wrapping her arms around Wendy, Nikki pulled her close. "It's all right. We knew something was wrong when he wasn't at home or at his office. When Hawk found out your husband had been killed in Atlantic City, I knew you were the next target."

"Am I going to jail?" Wendy cried.

"No," Nikki promised. "But a few people are. The FBI's on their way to town right now to arrest five people who Mayor Slokam has been protecting. They'll be going to jail together."

"So he'll be in jail with them...guess the creepy old man never got rid of the roaches after all," Wendy said and began laughing through her tears.

Confused, Nikki held Wendy in her arms.

17

Mr. and Mrs. Hochberg sipped hot tea from their mugs. Sitting at Nikki's kitchen table, they thanked her for the peace of mind they now had. "Oh, I didn't do much," Nikki admitted, brushing a piece of lint off the green dress she was wearing. "This case had a few twists and turns to it. There was a lot going on behind the curtains that I wasn't aware of. I did a whole lot of guessing."

"Your experience told you what path to follow," Johan corrected Nikki.

Smiling, Nikki admired the old man and how brilliant he looked in the brown suit he was wearing. Adal, even though old, sat wearing a lovely light brown dress that brought out her beautiful features. Feeling a fondness for the old couple, Nikki regretted that her time with them was coming to an end. "Can't you stay?" she begged.

"Our son was murdered in this village," Adal told Nikki,

sipping her tea, "so it is not good for us to remain here. You will come to Germany and visit us, yes?"

"Someday," Nikki promised. "I have my store to run, and if I don't call my son soon, he might send out a search party for me."

Johan sipped at his tea. "The people arrested, they were part of this Bonaduci family?"

"Yes, all five of them. Looks like the only medicine Dr. Mayton will be practicing will be in the prison hospital," Nikki explained. "Mayor Slokam was forced to protect those criminals against his will. Mrs. Slokam confessed a lot to Hawk. The Bonaducis were sent here from Boston because Mayor Slokam owed Mr. Bonaduci a favor. Seems like when they were young, Mayor Slokam got himself into some trouble, and Mr. Bonaduci helped him out of that trouble."

"Even in a small village such as this," Adal said sadly, "crime flourishes."

"What will happen to this Mayor Slokam?" Johan asked Nikki, putting down his tea. "And Mrs. Phillips, what is her fate?"

"Mayor Slokam will die in prison, and Wendy Phillips, due to the fine legal team she was able to hire, will not serve any jail time. In time, she will heal, but not here in Maple Hills. She has decided to move to Maine and be close to her cousin. I think that decision is for the best. I wanted to become her friend, but there is no life for her in Maple Hills anymore," Nikki explained to Johan. Reaching across the table, she patted his wrinkled hands. "You're such wonderful people. I am so sorry for your miseries."

"We all have our sorrows," Johan told Nikki, producing a weak smile. "It is time for us to go, yes? You will drive us to Boston, please."

"Of course," Nikki said, feeling her heart break. Standing up, she took her purse and walked the two broken-hearted old people out of her kitchen.

After returning from Boston, Nikki settled down on the couch and spent the rest of the night listening to a gentle rain fall outside. "I had to choose this town, didn't I? I wonder what's next." She yawned and slowly drifted off to sleep.

18

"You're all over the papers," Seth told his mother as he stood in a messy dorm room that smelled of dirty socks. Sitting down on an unmade bed, he pressed his cell phone up against his ear. "Mom, really, I can't leave you alone for a minute. Bonaduci family, German Mafia, murder...I thought you moved away from Atlanta to get away from all of that stuff!"

Sitting on the wooden bench in front of the duck pond, Nikki grinned at Hawk. "My son," she said, "he worries."

Nodding his head, Hawk looked out at the duck pond. Still wearing his same old t-shirt and blue jeans, he wondered how in the world he was going to get a beautiful woman who sat next to him dressed in a stylish pink and yellow dress to notice him. *Well,* Hawk thought, spotting the ducks, *what this woman needs is a friend, and I can be that.* "Did you tell him we're going to get married?" he joked.

"Married?!" Seth yelled.

Nikki rolled her eyes and took the call off of speaker

mode. "Detective Daily was only kidding. He's here having breakfast with me. We worked on the case together, and he needs a few statements from me for his files," Nikki explained and elbowed Hawk in the side. "Not funny," she mouthed.

Hawk grinned. He started to say something when his cell phone rang. "Excuse me," he told Nikki, standing up. Walking back toward the cabin, he answered the call. "Yeah, Detective Daily speaking...I see...no, I'll be right down, Pop."

Nikki watched Hawk stuff the cell phone down into the front pocket of his jeans. "Something the matter?" she asked when Hawk walked back to the bench.

Sitting down, Hawk pointed at the ducks with his eyes. "People say ducks are dumb, but I think they're pretty smart. Sitting in a pond all day, eating grass or small fish. No hassle, no traffic, no crime..."

"Mom...hey, Mom," Nikki heard her son yelling through the cell phone, "you still there? Hello?"

"Uh, Seth, let me call you right back, okay? I love you," Nikki said to him.

"Please, go inside, bake chocolate, charge tourists a lot of money, and wrinkle quietly," Seth begged. "I can't spend my time away at college worrying about you."

"I'm fine," Nikki promised. "I'll call you back in a minute."

"That was Pop," Hawk told Nikki, admiring the beauty of her backyard. "You're not going to believe this, Nikki, but a tourist was found dead in his room out at the Elk Horn Lodge." Shaking his head, Hawk looked at Nikki.

"What, why are you looking at me so strangely?" Nikki asked.

"Things were quiet before you arrived. What are you, a criminal magnet? First, it was this whole mess with Hanz Hochberg being run down, and now a tourist has been found dead. I tell you what, with you around it's never going to be dull."

"You'd rather I leave and go back to Atlanta?" Nikki asked, offended. Standing up she walked toward the duck pond. Hawk jumped up and followed.

"Hey, I didn't mean anything. I was... it was a bad joke, okay?" he apologized.

Turning to face Hawk, Nikki studied his face and found sincerity. "Hawk, my husband always put down my work. He never respected what I did because I was a woman. Now I don't claim to be Sherlock Holmes, but every time I figured out a crime, it made me feel like I was doing something worthwhile."

"Hey, you don't have to explain yourself to me—"

"Please, just listen," Nikki asked Hawk. "I had to leave Atlanta because everything became too political. Every step I took I had to take three steps backward. After a while—and especially after my divorce—it just didn't seem worth it anymore. And then I arrive here, and wow, I get pulled into some case. At first, I began my own investigation to protect myself, but then it became about helping people again, and that felt good."

Hawk stared into Nikki's sweet face. "I guess it did," he said and scratched the back of his head.

Nikki drew in a deep breath. "I'm going to keep my store

and bake my chocolate, but after much thought, I've decided to run my own investigative firm, from my cabin that is. I figured if I can make chocolate-covered strawberries, why not have a few chocolate-covered mysteries to go with them?"

"Well, I'll be," Hawk said, impressed with Nikki. "Pop sure isn't gonna like this news. No sir, not one bit. He's finally getting this town back to normal."

Nikki reached forward and looped her arm through Hawk's right arm. "I'm not worried about Chief Daily. All I'm interested in right now is this new case of ours."

"Now wait a minute, who said anything about you getting involved in this case?" Hawk asked. "I admit you have a pretty smart brain, but police work is police work, and we have rules to follow."

"Well, let me put it this way," Nikki said, walking Hawk to the duck pond. "I'm fed up with being told no. Consider me your silent partner...partner." And with that, Nikki shoved Hawk into the cold water of the duck pond.

Splashing, Hawk fought his way to the surface and spit pond water out of his mouth. Staring at Nikki, first in shock, and then in disbelief, he tried to make sense of her actions. "Okay, okay," he caved in, "you can help me out on some cases."

Nikki threw her hands onto her hips and shook her head.

"Okay, okay...all my cases," Hawk said and swam toward shore. "Will you help me out, partner?" he asked.

"Why sure," Nikki smiled. Reaching out her hands, she pulled Hawk out of the pond. "So," she said in an excited voice, "you handle the basics, and I'll do the digging around. I'll need you to tell me where the tourist was from, his age, his marital status, his profession..."

"Oh boy," Hawk said, feeling Nikki grab his arm and rush him around the cabin to his Jeep.

Back in the pond, the ducks waited until the humans were gone and resumed their normal lazy routine. Silly humans. They sure needed to learn to slow down and take it easy, smell the flowers and enjoy life in a small town.

ABOUT THE AUTHOR

Wendy Meadows is the USA Today bestselling author of many novels and novellas, from cozy mysteries to clean, sweet romances. Check out her popular cozy mystery series Sweetfern Harbor, Alaska Cozy and Sweet Peach Bakery, just to name a few.

If you enjoyed this book, please take a few minutes to leave a review. Authors truly appreciate this, and it helps other readers decide if the book might be for them. Thank you!

Get in touch with Wendy
www.wendymeadows.com

amazon.com/author/wendymeadows

goodreads.com/wendymeadows

bookbub.com/authors/wendy-meadows

facebook.com/AuthorWendyMeadows

twitter.com/wmeadowscozy

Copyright © 2017 by Wendy Meadows

All rights reserved.

No part of this publication may be reproduced, distributed or transmitted in any form or by any means, without prior written permission.

This is a work of fiction. Names, characters, places, and incidents are a product of the author's imagination. Locales and public names are sometimes used for atmospheric purposes. Any resemblance to actual people, living or dead, or to businesses, companies, events, institutions, or locales is completely coincidental.

Printed in the United States of America

Printed in Great Britain
by Amazon